THE SILENT SURROGATE

A PSYCHOLOGICAL SUSPENSE THRILLER

N. L. HINKENS

Text copyright @ 2019 Norma Hinkens

Published by Dunecadia Publishing, California

ISBN 978-1-947890-11-4

Cover by: www.derangeddoctordesign.com

Editing by: www.jeanette-morris.com/first-impressions-writing

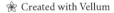 Created with Vellum

1

PRESENT DAY

*J*peer around the kitchen curtain of my new rental as a young woman in a leather mini-skirt exits the granny flat in my next-door-neighbors' backyard. A volcano of pink hair explodes from her head, the morning sun glinting off the piercings lurking in unexpected places in her flawless features. She throws a darting glance over her shoulder, her nose twitching above scowling, plum-colored lips, before striding off on long, lean legs into the chilly morning. I let the curtain slip back into place, shielding myself from view, the uneasy thud of my heart the only sound in the silence that envelops me. This is an unexpected twist, but I won't allow her to derail my plans. I'll make it my business to find out who she is and why she is living in my enemy's guest house.

I finish unpacking the box of dishes and Tupperware I left on the counter and make my way back out to my beat-up Nissan parked in the driveway.

A tall, good-looking man with a thick head of dark curls and a strong jawline strides up to me. I recognize him immediately. I've studied his picture on Facebook, but he's not the person I'm most interested in.

He extends an amicable hand in greeting. "I'm Rick West, welcome to the neighborhood. My wife, Lynn, and I live next door."

I recoil inwardly but allow him to squeeze my palm. I manage a tight smile in response. "Nora Munroe, nice to meet you." The name rolls comfortably off my lips. I settled on it after browsing baby name websites for days on end.

When Rick releases my hand, I reach into the trunk to lift out a box marked *miscellaneous kitchen supplies.*

"Here, let me get that for you." Without waiting for an answer, he hoists the battered cardboard box out with ease.

I shrug my thanks, swoop up an armful of clothing dangling precariously from an assortment of plastic hangers, and make my way up the front steps. After leading Rick down the narrow hallway to the kitchen, I gesture at the already overloaded table. "Just set it down anywhere you find a spot."

A female voice calls out from the front door. "Hel-lo! Anyone home?"

"Come on in," I echo back, as I drape the clothing over the back of a wooden chair. The kitchen in this rental is dated and the furniture scuffed, but I'm not complaining. The location couldn't be more perfect.

"This is my wife, Lynn," Rick says, as a short, brown-haired woman appears in the doorway bearing a platter of homemade cookies.

A dull gong sounds somewhere deep inside my chest. I've been preparing myself for this moment for a long time, but that doesn't make it any easier now that I'm face-to-face with the woman I've been hunting down for the past year. We exchange pleasantries, although I'd much rather stick a knife through her heart.

Lynn West is surprisingly plain, her hair limp around a narrow face harboring too-small eyes and thin lips that disappear into slits. She looks older than Rick, mid-thirties like me, I'm guessing. She's lucky to have landed such a handsome husband. And a younger one at that. I wonder what she did to deserve him. I'll make it my business to find out, of course. The more information I can gather, the more ways I will have to destroy her.

"Hope you're not averse to chocolate." Lynn laughs self-consciously and glances down at the decorative ceramic plate in her hand.

I flash her a faux-sympathetic smile. "Allergic, I'm afraid."

I'm not allergic to anything, as far as I know, but there's no way I'll ever eat a morsel that comes from that woman's hand.

She blinks, a tinge of red warming her cheeks. "I'll have to whip you up something else, I'm afraid. These are chocolate chip, heavy on the dairy."

"Don't worry about it," I simper back. "Sorry to be such a pain—first impressions and all that. They do look delicious. I hope they won't go to waste on my account."

Lynn swats her hand dismissively. "Not at all. Rick can take them with him to work tomorrow."

"I'm the youth program director at Garden Grove Community Center. It's in the rough part of town," he explains with a wink. "We live on sugar and caffeine."

"Wonderful," I mumble, trying to mask my surprise that he's pursuing such an altruistic vocation. I gathered from Facebook that he was a director of something or other but didn't give it much thought beyond that. I pictured him in the corporate environment hammering out deals over lunches and golf. He must have half the teens in his program swooning over him—their mothers too. I can't help wondering how Lynn feels about all the competition for her husband's attention. I turn an innocent gaze on her. "Do you work there too?"

"No, I'm a social worker. I work with the family court in Akron."

An iron fist tightens in my chest at her words, even though it's hardly news. Social services should have fired her after what happened under her watch. Instead, they let her transfer here and hide like the coward she is.

"That sounds interesting," I force out. "Challenging too, I bet."

"It's mostly custody disputes and abuse cases. It can be draining at times, but I love helping people. It's what I was made to do."

I give a mechanical smile in return, my lips barely cooperating. I'm under no such illusion. Hurting people is what she's really good at.

She sets down the plate and gestures to a mannequin leaning up against the couch. "Let me guess. You're a seamstress?"

I shake my head, shifting easily into my adopted persona. "Not a hope. I can't even sew on a button properly. I sell clothing online. The mannequin is for displaying the items I photograph for my website. It's easier than modeling everything myself and trying to take selfies at the same time." I pat my belly and arch a playful brow. "Besides, the mannequin's stomach is permanently flat, and I have to hold mine in." The truth is, I gained an extra twenty pounds I haven't been able to shake after my world imploded, thanks to her. But she doesn't need to know about the havoc she wreaked in my life, at least not yet. Not until I've accomplished what I came here to do.

"You'll have to show me your website once you're all moved in," Lynn gushes. "I'm intrigued."

"Sure, I'd love to." I took the precaution of actually

building a website in case anyone asked to see it. It's not functional—no working E-commerce back end or anything like that. But, if all goes according to plan, I won't be here long enough for anyone to see through the illusion.

"Honey, we should probably get out of here and leave Nora to finish unpacking." Lynn glances uncertainly at her husband and then back to me. "Unless there's something we can help you with? Do you need anything moved in?"

"No, I'm all set, thanks. The place came furnished. I just need to figure out where I want to put things." I gesture at the plate of cookies. "Don't forget your goodies."

Lynn makes an apologetic face and swoops up her plate. "I'll bring you over a dairy-free offering some other time."

"If you need anything at all, we're just next door—the white house with the green trim," Rick adds with another irritating wink. He's obviously used to commanding all the attention. Little does he know it's his wife I'm interested in. He raises his hand in a parting wave and follows her out of the kitchen and back down the hallway. After they pull the front door closed behind them, I slip into the family room and watch them walk across the lawn to their house, Lynn balancing her plate of cookies like the evil queen with her poisoned apple. I know what lurks beneath her do-gooder veneer. There's something about him I don't like either—he's too slick for his own good. But as long as he doesn't ask too many questions, we'll get along just fine until the time is right to make my move.

2

FEBRUARY 09, 2008

I'm hiding in the basement like a criminal. I told you I was going down to clean out the freezer. Not that you really notice when I'm gone, or care what I spend my time doing anymore. You only have one thing on your mind.

My fingers are shaking so hard I can barely hold this pen. There's a part of me that doesn't want to commit my thoughts to paper. I've been fighting the idea for a long time. Yet, here I am scribbling down my dark secrets, as if this will fix everything that's wrong in my life.

I'm worried that someday someone will stumble across this journal and find out just how broken I am inside because of what you're doing. I think I've been pretty good at hiding the truth from our circle of family and friends. Even the neighbors are oblivious to what's going on inside our four walls. But hiding it is not something to be proud of. It's time to pull my head out of the sand and face the frightening reality I've been avoiding for months. This is my life now, and I have to own it.

Okay, I'm rambling, unsure of where to begin. All I know is that I need to do this—come clean on paper, at least. For you, for me, for Jonathan. To be honest I doubt if our relationship can be salvaged at this point. It depends on how willing you are to put in the hard work that needs to be done. Based on what I've seen so far, I'm not holding out much hope of anything changing. So, everything I do from this day forward will be with Jonathan's best interests in mind. I want him to know that one day. That's why keeping this journal—this hard evidence of my efforts—is so important.

I still remember clearly the magical moment when our son was born. We barely made it to the hospital in time. There was an accident, a fatality, and the road into town was blocked off. A police officer on the scene escorted us through the barricade when he saw our predicament. It stormed hard all that morning, raindrops drumming relentlessly against the window. But right after Jonathan popped out, the sun burst through the iron-gray sky and spilled into our hospital room, bathing his face in an otherworldly light. We both cried euphoric sobs mingled with tears of relief that our son was finally here, and healthy all the way down to his ten perfect toes—yes, I counted them twice to make sure. Even some of the nurses were dabbing at the corners of their eyes, moved by the finger of sunlight tracing its way across Jonathan's forehead like an angelic blessing. It was a spiritual moment, one that held such promise, a promise that now feels broken.

3

....

PRESENT DAY

I'm walking to the post office the next morning to mail the final payment to the PI I hired to help me track down Lynn West, when a slight, gray-haired woman walking an overweight, chocolate-and-tan dachshund stops me.

"You must be Nora Munroe, our new neighbor. Rick and Lynn told me all about you. I'm Annie Edmonds. I live four doors down from you in the house with the cherry blossoms." Her lips pucker in an apologetic grimace. "The one with the untidy garden. It's been so hard to keep it up since my Frank passed away last year." She frowns, her rheumy eyes glistening in the morning sun. "He died of pancreatic cancer. A terrible way to go. I wouldn't wish it on anyone."

When she pauses long enough to take a breath, I indulge her with a commiserative smile. Her loss is nothing in comparison to mine, but I have no intention of divulging the harrowing details of what I've been through to a stranger. I already beat it to death during my mandatory therapy sessions with Doctor Miller. Talking didn't help. I'm done talking—it's time to do something, which is why I came here.

8

"It's nice to meet you, Annie," I say, leaning down to pet her dog. For the most part I prefer dogs to people. They don't screw up your life the way people do, especially the ones who like to meddle, like Lynn West. "I'm so sorry about your husband."

"Thank you, dear." She throws a curious glance at the envelope in my hand. "Perhaps you'd like to stop by for a cup of tea? After you've mailed your letter." The forlorn note in her voice resonates in the air between us.

I do a quick assessment. Elderly, lonely, likes to prattle. Annie Edmonds could prove to be a useful source of information on my new neighbors. And I may need an unwitting accomplice when the time comes. It's a relationship worth exploring. "That would be lovely, Annie," I reply. "I'll see you in a few minutes."

As it turns out, the post office is packed, and I stand in line for a good fifteen minutes before I reach the counter. It doesn't bother me in the least. It gives me a chance to listen in on several conversations between customers as the line slowly winds back and forth between the ropes guiding us to our destination. By the time I pay for my stamps and exit the post office, I'm armed with an interesting tidbit of my own to share with the inquisitive Annie Edmonds. Something that I'm guessing is fresh off the neighborhood rumor mill and will serve to cement our fledgling friendship.

Annie wasn't exaggerating about the neglected state of her garden. Unkempt and overgrown, plants ramble in myriad directions, just like she does the minute she opens her mouth. I unlatch the white, wrought-iron gate, ignoring its creak of protest, and make my way up the flagstone path to the front door. As I raise my hand to ring the doorbell, I catch sight of Annie waving at me through the picture window on the left. I wave back, adjusting the strap of my purse on my shoulder as I wait for her to make an appearance. A moment later, the door opens, and she ushers me over the threshold into a gloomy hallway hung with faded family photos in formulaic poses.

"I'm so happy you could make it," Annie gushes. "I was just saying to Rick the other week how nice it would be to have the house on the corner rented out again. It's been lying vacant for months, and it always makes me nervous having an empty property nearby. Next thing you know, you have squatters and drug dealers and all sorts of strange folks coming and going at all hours." She banters on as she leads me down the hallway to a cluttered kitchen where she proceeds to shoo an overweight cat out of a chair. "Sit right down while I pop the kettle on. Would you prefer tea or coffee?"

"Tea would be great," I say, eying the floral tieback cushion on the chair dubiously. I contemplate untying it and flipping it so I don't end up covered in cat hair, but it wouldn't be prudent to offend Annie right off the bat on my first visit to her home. I need her on my side, at least until I determine how useful she might be.

I perch on the edge of the cushion and give the cat an obnoxious glare, but it continues to stare back at me as if contemplating jumping into my lap out of sheer spite. Unnerved, I scoot my chair under the table to avoid any possibility of feline contact.

"Where's your cute little dachshund?" I ask, darting a meaningful glance around the room. Maybe the dog's appearance will be enough to send the cat skulking out of here.

"Daisy?" Annie chuckles as she reaches for a tray and loads up two china mugs and a gilt-trimmed plate piled high with muffins. "Little tyrant. Always digging up my pansy beds. She's not mine. I walk her whenever I can for my friend, Charles. He has arthritis, and he has a hard time getting around without his cane. The doctor says he needs a new knee but he's stubborn, that one. He's holding out as long as he can."

I try not to look too disappointed at the news that Daisy won't be coming to my rescue any time soon.

Annie sighs. "My Frank was the same way when it came to doctors." She sets the tray on the table and sinks into the chair next to me. "If only he'd gone to see one sooner, he might have had a fighting chance." Before she can begin unloading the tray, the cat leaps up into her lap. Annie smiles down at it and strokes its head affectionately. "This is my little lovebug, Leo. He's a Persian longhair."

I wrack my brains for something complimentary to say about the shaggy predator extending and retracting its claws in a threatening manner, its slit-eyed gaze firmly fixed on me.

"Leo," I echo. "That's … a great name for a cat."

He licks his paw as though savoring the compliment. Or maybe he's imagining the taste of my blood. He looks like he has slasher tendencies.

Annie smiles as she hands me a mug. "Sugar? Or I have honey if you prefer?"

"No, thank you." I peer down at the amber liquid to make sure there are no stray cat hairs bobbing on the surface. It has a peculiar odor, like some kind of herbal tea, but I'll suffer through it.

"Where did you move from?" Annie asks, stirring a generous helping of sugar into her tea.

"Philadelphia." It's close enough to the truth to be able to bluff my way through any questions Annie, or anyone else, might throw my way. I grew up on the outskirts of Philadelphia, but I haven't been there in a long time. I don't dare disclose where I've been living for the past decade—just in case someone has read about my story and connects the dots.

"Oh my, Philadelphia's a big city." Annie passes the plate of muffins which I politely decline. There's no way I can be sure they are free and clear of Slasher's hair without biting into one. Annie reaches for a muffin and peels off the paper cup. "So, what brings you to Akron?"

I tighten my grip on the handle of my mug as a variety of plausible reasons flash to mind. Anonymity, a fresh start, strange faces who don't know my past and won't pity me. The real reason, of course, is revenge. Lynn West took everything from me, and I intend to make sure she pays for what she did. "Work," I answer. "I sell clothing online. My supplier is based in Ohio."

"How exciting, dear! Mind you, I can't imagine buying clothes online myself. I mean, how can you be sure they fit? And I like to feel the material between my fingers to make sure the quality's good."

"I sell brand names," I explain, launching into the verbiage I garnered from the internet. "Typically, people are familiar with the brands that fit them well. And I offer free return shipping, so people can try things on in the comfort of their homes before committing to a purchase." The phrases flow smoothly and make me sound like I know what I'm talking about. In reality, I've never worked a day in retail. "What about you, Annie? I assume you're retired?"

"Yes, I was a pediatric nurse. I've been retired for close to ten years now. I did some volunteer work for a couple of years after that at Garden Grove Community Center—where your next-door neighbor, Rick West, works—until it all got to be too much for me."

I arch a brow, sensing an opportunity to glean a little more information about the Wests. "Rick must have all the volunteers falling over themselves to work his shift. How on earth did Lynn manage to snag such a handsome husband?"

Annie sips on her tea, as though considering her answer.

"I guess you could say she saved him. Rick was a heavy drinker in high school, dabbling in drugs, going down the same path as his father before him. Lynn is eight years older than Rick. She was working at the family court when she met him. Turned him right around, she did. He's been clean and sober ever since."

I digest the news in silence. So she married a junkie. Lynn likes to think she can rescue people—reform them even. But I know better than most that a leopard never changes its spots.

MARCH 02, 2008

ere I am again, stuck for words like a stubborn gearshift that won't budge into drive. I'm not good at this. My plan was to write something every day. Even if it was only a couple of lines. I thought it would be a healthy way to take stock of my feelings, but mostly that it would be useful to document everything for Jonathan's sake. I hoped the process would be cathartic, but so far, I haven't been able to bring myself to write a single word since my first entry. My brain is fried, and my emotions have been all over the place like a slippery eel. Rising on a tide of hope that things are finally getting better, then sinking into a pit of despair that nothing is changing and never will. It's almost as if writing it all down is admitting failure. That's nonsense, of course, but somehow it feels less tangible when it's not committed to paper. Maybe we're both in denial.

Today was one of those rare days when I dared to hope, for a few precious moments, that everything will turn out all right after all. We took Jonathan to the park to feed the ducks after his afternoon nap. It's been weeks since we've gone out on a family walk or outing. I was cautiously optimistic. You pushed the stroller and I had Bella on the leash. A picture-perfect family to the naked eye.

Jonathan chattered away happily the entire time, pointing at the ducklings and clapping his hands as they glided through the water in their mother's wake. As for you, you were happier than I've seen you in a long time. You were laughing, Jonathan was laughing, I was laughing, at least on the outside. On the inside I was questioning everything. Is this real? Will this last? How can I believe in us anymore when my trust has been eroded?

And then you reached for Jonathan's arms and started spinning him around in circles, twirling him so fast my heart almost stopped.

"Be careful!" I yelled, my hands involuntarily flying out to reach for our son.

You turned to me and smiled. "He's fine, relax!"

Right on cue, Jonathan shrieked in delight and waved a chubby hand in my direction.

I forced myself to push away my doubts and embrace the moment, to savor the sight of our son basking in his parents' love, delighting in life's simple-but-treasured moments.

I chose to smile back at you then, even though my stomach was in knots. A smile that told you I believed in us, that I was committed to what we have together. The truth, is I'm floundering around in a no-man's land of fear and uncertainty, lurching forward one moment, falling backward the next, unable to make a decision of any real conviction about what to do. That's another reason I started writing down my thoughts. To try and process exactly how I feel and figure out what steps to take next. Maybe when I read back over these words, my path forward will become clearer.

On the one hand, journaling all of this feels like a betrayal of sorts—a betrayal of us. But I know that's illogical. You're the one who has betrayed us. You're the one who's been keeping secrets. And they're much bigger than the sin of a secret diary.

PRESENT DAY

"Would you like a refill, dear?" Annie asks, motioning to my half-full mug.

I hesitate, wondering if it's worth suffering through another few mouthfuls in a bid to extract some information about the young woman I saw exiting my neighbors' granny flat yesterday.

"Sure," I say with a sheepish grin. "So long as I'm not taking up too much of your time."

"Nonsense!" Annie retorts, her eyes crinkling with delight. "I'm glad of the company, and it's always nice to meet new people. I've been lonesome since my Frank passed away. He was such a good conversationalist. He always kept up with the news, so I never had to read the paper—he'd fill me in on everything going on in the world while I puttered around the kitchen making us a bite to eat. My eyesight's terrible now so even reading a book is difficult for me these days. I tried those audiobooks one time, but it's just not the same thing, is it?"

I make an appropriate sound to convey my agreement. I can't concentrate long enough to read a sentence anymore, let alone a book. I stopped taking the pills Doctor Miller prescribed a long time ago. They weren't helping. The only thing that will help is to make my enemy pay for what she did.

Annie shoos Leo out of her lap and scurries across the floor to put the kettle on again to boil. Leo arches his back and stalks past me, tail swaying disdainfully.

"Did you get your letter mailed?" Annie pins an expectant gaze on me.

I have a sneaking suspicion she's more interested in the contents of my letter than whether or not I mailed it. Time for a diversionary piece of gossip before I take our chat in a more productive direction.

"Yes, thanks. Which reminds me, a woman in the post office told me that a local ER doctor was arrested last night for a DUI." I actually overheard the conversation while standing in line, but my version makes me sound like the type of woman people confide in—the type of person a lonely soul like Annie can open up to.

She tuts her disapproval as she fills our mugs with hot water. "That's a real shame. Barnes Memorial Hospital has such a great reputation. Did you happen to catch the doctor's name?"

I rub my temple as if trying to recollect it, although I made a point of memorizing it. "Let's see, I think his last name was Phillips. Dane … no, Derek, that's it. Derek Phillips."

Annie lets out a horrified bleat as she sets down the kettle. "Phillips! I know his mother. Oh my, that is a shocker. Who would ever have thought that Lana Phillips' son would be arrested for drinking and driving? She was always so proud of him going off to medical school. It just goes to show, doesn't it?"

I murmur in agreement, although I'm not at all sure what

she thinks it shows—addiction's hardly a class problem, as I'm only too painfully aware. It's not a subject I want to dwell on. Time to steer the conversation back around to my next-door neighbors.

Annie shuffles across to the table with fresh mugs of tea. I pick mine up and interlock my fingers around it. "I noticed a young woman coming out of the flat at the back of the Wests' house yesterday," I venture, before nonchalantly taking a fresh sip. It's worse than the first cup, she's barely doused the teabag in the water—distracted by my DUI story, no doubt.

"Oh, you must mean Jessica. Dyed pink hair, rings and things all over."

"Yes, that's her! Is she visiting or something? She looks too old to be their daughter."

Annie chuckles. "She's only eight years younger than Rick. Jessica still dresses like a teenager but, believe it or not, she just turned twenty-one. She was such a beautiful girl when she was little—a real knockout as they used to say back in the day. I've no idea why she had to go and get all those piercings done. It's so unsightly. Trust me, that girl is nothing but trouble."

I raise my brows, waiting for Annie to elaborate as I know she is only too eager to do.

She swallows a mouthful of tea and then leans back in her chair studying me with an anticipatory air. "Jessica was in the youth program over at the community center years ago. Her father's in prison for armed robbery and her mother took off when she was a baby—could be dead for all anyone knows—so Jessica didn't have much parental guidance growing up. She was in and out of the foster system. She adored Rick though, worshipped the ground he walked on—I think she was half in love with him, to tell you the truth. She craved attention, and he gave it to her. When she turned eighteen, she moved away. No one knew where she was, but there were all sorts of rumors about drinking and drugs and stuff."

I drop my gaze. My hands begin to shake so hard I'm forced to set my mug back down on the table, the beige liquid slopping over the side and pooling on the plastic floral tablecloth. A dull rage stirs inside me, a familiar monster awakening from sleep.

"Anyway, she showed back up here right before Christmas and moved in with some pothead she met at a bar," Annie prattles on, oblivious to the turbulent emotions ricocheting through me. "Then a couple of months later, he kicked her out in the middle of the night and threw all her clothes into the street. She had nowhere to go, so Rick offered her a place to stay until she got on her feet again. They're good that way, helping out with the youth and all. Lynn never likes to give up on anyone, always gives them the benefit of the doubt, and Rick's sympathetic to their plight too after the battle he fought with addiction himself."

The anger simmering within me threatens to explode. Snippets of memories crash and collide inside my head. I can't believe her gall. How dare Lynn marry a junkie and house another one under her roof after what happened? She knows they can't be trusted. She vouched for my husband—gave him one chance too many, and it cost me everything.

"They sound like very caring people," I say, forcing the words from my lips as the room spins around me. Leo's kaleidoscopic eyes stare me down as if he knows the dark thoughts I'm thinking and why I really came here.

"They certainly are a kindhearted couple. Everyone thinks highly of them and what they do for the community. Rick even gave Jessica a part-time kitchen job at Garden Grove. Although, between you and me, he's a little too smooth for my liking—he does like to flirt with all the girls.

But, in his defense, I have to say when my Frank was poorly, Rick came around almost every day and … "

Annie's voice fades into the background as I lose myself in my churning thoughts. Despite the piercings and the dyed hair, Jessica is a stunning young woman. And if she had a crush on Rick in the past, why on earth would Lynn invite temptation into their home? She might be a believer in second chances, but something strikes me as off about the situation. I reach for my mug again, relieved to see that my fingers are no longer trembling. I need to calm down and think this through. If there's more to the story, it might turn out to be something I can use. "I take it Jessica's boyfriend doesn't want anything more to do with her?"

Annie purses her lips as she reaches for a second muffin. "Lynn told me he's a complete loser, that one." She leans forward conspiratorially and lowers her voice as though someone might hear us through the walls. "Jessica won't talk about him. She's acting very cagey about the whole situation, if you ask me. Mind you, it must have been embarrassing for her, poor thing, picking her underwear up off the street like that. After all, she grew up here and everyone knows her."

I nod distractedly. A lodger coming and going next door complicates things. I didn't anticipate Rick and Lynn having someone living with them. Still, it's no secret druggies can be bought for the right price. I'll find a way to get rid of Jessica.

"To be honest, I'm surprised Lynn agreed to let Jessica move in at all," I say, painting on a concerned expression. "I mean, Lynn seems like a nice enough person but, let's face it, she's not exactly what you'd call a looker, and Jessica's extremely attractive."

Leo leaps up into Annie's lap again and she rubs his neck. "Well, I don't disagree with you there. My generation wouldn't have entertained the idea, but folks nowadays have all sorts of living arrangements. I prefer to stay out of other people's business, leave well alone, so to speak."

I don't bother responding to that. Most busybodies are under the same misconception. Besides, I don't want to alienate Annie. I'm going to need her more than ever now that there's a lodger living next door. Two people I can handle, but three's a crowd.

6

MARCH 10, 2008

I wondered why you suddenly agreed to a family outing after shutting us out for weeks on end. I figured out you were high that day at the park, spinning around with Jonathan dangling by his arms. Of course he was happy—he's two years old, totally oblivious to the danger he was in. You made it all seem so lighthearted and fun, like I was the killjoy. But it's a dangerous game you're playing. You were being completely reckless. If you had tripped, or accidentally let go of Jonathan, he could have been badly injured. It's a miracle you didn't dislocate his shoulder. I can't be a neutral bystander any longer, not when you're putting our child's life in jeopardy!

Do you have any idea how hard it is to write those words? It's not just about us. You can't expect me to go along with this anymore.

I've had my suspicions for some time—like last Christmas when you slept until after four in the afternoon instead of watching Jonathan open his gifts from Santa. You were so clever at hiding it from me, for the most part. You certainly don't look like the typical strung-out, sack-of-bones druggie. You work out, your skin always looks good, and your eyes are as bright and beautiful as ever to me.

Yes, they still make me go weak at the knees. I can't spot any of the telltale signs they warn you to look for. You've never missed a day of work—you're very proud of that. They call people like you "high-functioning addicts" in the stack of pamphlets I've collected on the dangers of opioid addiction. I've read them all several times over, although you won't even crack one open no matter how many I leave lying accidentally-on-purpose in your pile of mail on the counter. These days I devour everything I can on the subject, as if by osmosis of enough information I might be able to cure you. It's amazing the crazy thoughts that come into my head in my desperation to avoid the inevitable.

In retrospect, the only thing I remember that might have been considered a red flag was that you didn't sleep much, especially after Jonathan was born. When the doctor prescribed a sedative, I was fully on board, completely unaware it would only add to the growing problem you were hiding from everyone, including me. Yes, you were careless and lost prescriptions here and there that had to be refilled, but I put it down to the fact that we had a newborn at home. We were in survival mode in those early months. Granted, you were a bit paranoid at times about anything happening to Jonathan, but we were first-time doting parents. We still are. I know, deep down, you adore our son. He's the light of our lives. Truth be told, we're probably both a bit over-protective of him. Except now I have reason to be. I used to love watching the two of you together. Now, I'm scared to leave him alone with you.

7

PRESENT DAY

*I*t's been three days since I moved into 23 Wilshire Place, and I'm already making inroads into winning my enemy's trust. Rick and Lynn have just popped over to ask me to help out at an event at the community center this morning.

"We're always short-handed in the kitchen on these kinds of occasions," Rick explains, shaking his dark hair out of his melted-chocolate eyes as he layers on the guilt. "Even Lynn pitches in. She usually oversees the hospitality side of things while my assistant, Jeff, helps me out with the ceremony. We're presenting our drug awareness program graduates with certificates of merit, and we're hosting a little celebration with the families afterward."

"It would be a great way for you to get to know some new people," Lynn urges.

I give her a deferential smile. "I'd love to help out. Give me a few minutes to get changed and then I'll head over there."

"Wonderful! See you soon," Rick says, with a parting wave.

The truth is I'm not interested in getting to know any more new people from the community. I've already identified everyone I need for my plan. The only reason I've agreed to go is because Annie mentioned that Jessica works part-time in the community center kitchen. I've been waiting for a chance to talk to her and feel her out. If anyone can give me insight into my enemy's world, it's someone who lives in it.

After trying on and discarding several outfits, I settle on a pair of skinny jeans and an oversized checked shirt that's similar to an outfit I've seen Jessica wearing. If I dress her age, she might be more inclined to gossip with me about her hosts.

By the time I get there, the community center is already hopping with families gathering in the main hall for the award ceremony—all scrubbed up and decked out in their finery for the occasion. Even the younger kids are dressed in shiny shoes, frilly dresses and button-down shirts. I weave my way through the throng of people to the kitchen in the back.

Lynn greets me with an exuberant, "Nora! I'm so glad you're here. We're rushed off our feet." She thrusts an empty pitcher into my hands and gestures to a beverage cooler. "Can you finish filling the lemonade pitchers and then set them out on the tables in the dining room, please?"

I cast a quick glance around the stainless-steel commercial kitchen, but there's no sign of Jessica anywhere. I hope Annie wasn't mistaken about her working here. I'm not excited about the prospect of wasting a morning volunteering for a philanthropic community cause under Lynn's direction, but for now it appears I'm stuck with it. I grit my teeth and set about filling the lemonade pitchers stacked ten-deep on the counter.

I'm carrying a tray of lemonade out to the tables when I spot Jessica slinking in a side door as she slips a weed pipe into her pocket. I freeze in place, the hair on the back of my neck rising. Do the Wests know their lodger is still doing dope? She throws a disinterested glance my way, working a wad of gum around her jaw as she struts across the hall in a short tartan skirt, black leggings and knee-high motorcycle boots. I finish placing the pitchers around the tables and retreat to the kitchen. To my relief, Lynn is nowhere in sight. Jessica has donned an apron and is standing at a counter stacked with loaves of sandwich bread and condiments. An older woman sets a tray of cheeses and assorted meats down next to her. She says something to Jessica and then walks off to the far end of the kitchen to help another volunteer unload cupcakes from Tupperware containers.

I sidle over next to Jessica and reach for a loaf of bread. "Hi, I'm Nora." I give her a fleeting smile, nothing too intrusive. "I've been asked to help you make the sandwiches." Without waiting for a response, I tear open the first bag and begin stacking slices of bread on the cutting board. "We can tag team this if you want. How about I do the condiments and you add the fillings?"

Jessica raises a stenciled brow and looks me slowly up and down. Her eyes are a piercing blue framed by long, thickly coated lashes. It's slightly unnerving standing this close to someone so beautiful. I can't see a single pore in her creamy skin. It's easy to imagine how her classic cheekbones and the curve of her lush lips make for an intoxicating combination to any man who falls under her spell. But her looks won't last if she continues down the path she's on.

"You live next door, don't you?" she says, adjusting her apron.

"That's right. I moved in a few days ago." I unscrew the lid on the catering-sized jar of mayonnaise and begin slathering the slices on the cutting board, listening to the irritating smacking sound of Jessica working her gum around her mouth. Annie was right about her acting like a teenager, in more ways than one.

She pulls the platter of cheese and assorted meats closer and reaches for a few pieces. "Where'd you move from?"

I open a tub of mustard and add a dollop to each slice. "Philadelphia, how about you?"

After a slight hesitation, Jessica responds. "I grew up here. I've lived all over."

I keep my head down, pretending to concentrate on keeping the condiments inside the crusts, not wanting to appear overly interested in her past. She's the suspicious sort, like junkies typically are—a paranoia I understand only too well.

"Did you move here for work?" Jessica asks, adding a generous helping of meat and cheese to each slice of bread before slapping the sandwiches closed.

"Yes, I have an online clothing store. My supplier's based here in Akron." I gesture at my outfit. "This came from my store."

Jessica raises her brows. "I'd like to try doing something like that. Beats this crappy job. What's your website called?"

"*Raven Streetwear.*"

"Cool name." Jessica spins the platter of meats and cheeses and grabs several more slices.

"Thanks, I thought it had a good ring to it." I don't add that according to Wikipedia, ravens are associated with bad luck, so the name seemed especially fitting. Lynn West doesn't realize it yet, but her luck ran out when I rented the house next door to her.

"I can show you my online store once we're done here if you like," I offer, careful to keep my tone nonchalant.

Jessica shrugs. "Yeah, whatever." She lifts a bread knife and begins cutting the sandwiches diagonally.

I suppress the tiniest of grins as I open another loaf. A

connection has been made. I have a mole in my enemy's camp.

8

MARCH 28, 2008

*D*ropping hints about the potential dangers of your behavior and where it could lead to has got me nowhere. You shut me down, or brush off my concerns, acting as if I'm the crazy one for being such a worrywart. You keep insisting your idealized version of everything will work out. But the facts about addiction don't lie. I read that over seventy-thousand people die every year from accidental overdoses involving prescription opioids. Even if you don't kill yourself, the long-term prognosis isn't good—paranoia, depression, aggression, hallucinations—I've already seen the signs. I lie awake at night and worry about all of these things while you're doped up on sleeping pills.

So, tonight, I changed tactics. I decided to have a lengthy sit-down conversation with you over dinner about what's been going on. It didn't go well. You barely touched your steak and salad. (I even went to the trouble of cooking your favorite meal. The one you stared at and pushed around on your plate while I talked.) You flat out told me you weren't in the mood for food or conversation. I know you were itching for a fix the entire time, especially as I didn't put any wine out on the table. I wanted your full attention.

For once, I didn't dance around the topic. I told you it had to stop or else I was going to leave you. I broached it in a loving manner, stressing how much I loved you and couldn't bear the thought of anything happening to you. I even pulled out our wedding album and Jonathan's baby book, and made you look through them with me. I thought I could hold it together but I couldn't keep the tremor out of my voice.

You remained unmoved. I told you I didn't want to have to face the thought of raising our son alone as a single parent. That I wanted us to be a team again. At one point, I almost got down on my knees and begged you to get help before I found myself kneeling at your graveside. But for all my dramatic posturing, I didn't get through to you. You said I was being ridiculous, it would never come to that—that you had everything under control.

But I know better. I've read the pamphlet that talks about the lies addicts tell themselves. Denial is a dangerous place to live, a mirage that melts away too late to save the unlucky souls it lures to destruction.

9

PRESENT DAY

*W*hen we've finished making ample stacks of sandwiches for the luncheon, Jessica and I join the other volunteers at the back of the main hall and listen in on the tail end of Rick's speech to the graduates and their families. He's a compelling speaker and the crowd remains riveted while he regales them with amusing anecdotes from the various teambuilding and self-awareness activities the kids engaged in during the course of the program. His assistant, Jeff, stands to one side, clutching a bundle of certificates and a box of medals to be distributed to each of the participants. Jessica is completely caught up in the performance, unabashedly basking in Rick's silver-tongued wit and arresting looks as he grasps the podium and addresses the crowd, dressed in a gray suit and baby blue tie.

At the conclusion of his speech, he presents each graduate with a certificate and distributes several merit awards, before closing the ceremony and inviting everyone to join the graduates in the dining room for sandwiches, cupcakes, and lemonade.

For the next half hour or so, I make myself useful passing

around trays of food, refilling pitchers, cleaning up cupcake remnants trodden underfoot, and clearing away plates. The cavernous room is an echo chamber of crying babies, sugar-crazed kids running amok, and raucous laughter, and it takes all my willpower not to drop everything and make a beeline for the exit. I don't like crowds—or people in general—and it's harder than ever to pass myself off now that I've given up my medication. But, if nothing else, I'm ingratiating myself with the community and that will work in my favor when it comes time to enact my plan. When I reach Rick's table, he gets to his feet and introduces me to his assistant. "Jeff, meet my new neighbor, Nora Munroe."

Jeff shakes my hand, a befuddled look flickering momentarily across his face. "You look … familiar. Have we met before?"

I give a nervous laugh. "You must be thinking of someone else. I only moved here recently." Heart pounding merci-lessly, I turn my attention to the rest of the table and hold up the pitcher in my hand. "More lemonade, anyone?" My thoughts race in myriad directions as I busy myself refilling a couple of plastic tumblers. Was it purely a coincidence, or did Jeff really recognize me? Surely, he couldn't have connected the rail-thin, disheveled blonde on the news five years ago with the slightly overweight woman with the sleek, black bob whom Rick just introduced him to.

"Nora! Come over here and meet Charles." I turn in the direction of Annie's voice to see her waving me over to her table. Seated next to her is an elderly gentleman with a neat, white mustache and a glistening bald spot on his head. An aluminum walking cane is folded neatly beneath his chair.

Annie beams at me as I join them. "This is Daisy's owner, my good friend, Charles Atkins. Charles, this is Nora Munroe. Remember I told you she moved into the vacant house at the end of the street?"

Charles gets to his feet with difficulty and stretches out a marbled blue-and-purple hand for me to shake. I set down my tray and give his hand a perfunctory squeeze. "Pleased to meet you, Charles. I love your little dachshund."

He bobs his head in acknowledgement. "Feel free to stop by anytime. Daisy loves anyone who's willing to make a fuss over her. Annie can bring you by. I live on Ash Drive, the next street over. And if you like tomatoes, I can send you home with some from my garden. I have more than I can possibly use at the moment."

"Ooh," Annie coos. "Charles is a dab hand at growing tomatoes. I bet you've never tasted any half as good as his. He swears by that organic fish fertilizer he uses but it's really down to his green thumb."

"Thank you, Charles, that's very kind of you," I say, reaching for my tray. "I'll make a point of coming by soon."

I move on to the next table and begin gathering up the discarded plates. I don't need to make any more friends, but I genuinely like Daisy, and Charles might turn out to have his uses. One visit can't do any harm. At the very least, it will keep me in Annie's good graces if I pay her crippled friend a visit.

By the time the last families have vacated the dining hall, the tables and chairs are folded and stacked, and the floor is swept, I'm physically wiped out and mentally burned out on social interaction. To my dismay, Jessica squeezes my arm in passing as I'm heading for the main exit doors.

"I'm almost done helping Lynn in the kitchen," she informs me. "I'll drop by and check out your clothing website once I get back."

"Great," I say, trying to muster up some enthusiasm. I need to make the most of this opportunity now that I've hooked her interest. "See you in a bit."

. . .

AN HOUR LATER, Jessica finally shows up on my doorstep. I was too tired to shower but I did manage to get in a ten-minute power nap. It's important that I make every effort to forge a friendship with Jessica. She can act as my proverbial fly on the wall next door until I figure out a way to get rid of her. I usher her inside and offer her a glass of wine. A test of sorts. Annie said she was trouble. I want to know just how true the rumors are, and what her weaknesses are.

I can tell by the longing look in her eyes that she considers it for a moment. Then, to my surprise, she curls her lip and shakes her head. "Better not. I'm trying to stay off the booze."

"Oh?" I look at her inquiringly.

She laughs. "I went off the rails for a bit. It's a long story. I'm attempting to live clean as long as I'm bunking with Rick and Lynn." She rolls her eyes. "One of their conditions."

I sense she's keeping something from me—her drug use, or something else? Whatever it is, she's not ready to open up to me yet.

"How about a soda?" I suggest. "Or juice?"

"Just a water for me, please. No ice."

I retreat to the kitchen and fill a glass with water, debating as to which direction I should steer the conversation next. I want to know more about who she is and why Lynn took her in. But I'll have to tread carefully and make Jessica feel as if she's choosing to confide in me. The last thing I need is for her to clam up.

"Here you go," I say, handing her the water.

"Cheers." Jessica leans back against the cushions and makes herself comfortable. "So, how'd you get into selling clothes online?"

I shrug. "It sort of evolved. I tried a couple of different home-based businesses before I opened my online store. I do a mixture of new and secondhand items, all brand name stuff, so it has good resale value."

"I should give that a shot," Jessica muses. "I'm into fashion, and everyone tells me I have an eye for it." She takes a swig of water and sets down her glass. "Let's take a look."

I retrieve my laptop from the built-in shelving unit on the far wall and sit down next to Jessica on the couch. After the computer powers up, I click on my bookmarked website.

"Wow!" Jessica's eyes widen as the photos load. "It looks very professional."

Considering the fact that I spent almost a week perfecting it, it's reassuring to hear that I've hit the mark. "If you're interested in any items, I can let you have them at cost."

Jessica lets out a snort of laughter and then tries to cover it up. "Sorry, I didn't mean to be rude. I love your clothes. It's nice of you to offer and all. It's just that ... "

I let out an exaggerated gasp. "No, *I'm* sorry, that was thoughtless of me. I wasn't trying to bag a sale or anything. You probably don't have any extra money if you're working at the community center part-time."

"It's not that." Jessica falls silent for a moment, and then sighs. "You're going to find out soon enough anyway. It's just that I—*we*—haven't told anyone yet." She runs a hand through her fluffy, pink hair. "The thing is, I'm four-and-a-half months pregnant."

Dumbfounded, I stare at her. Questions whip around my head in quick succession. Do Rick and Lynn know? Is that why they took her in? Is it her ex's baby?

"Wow!" I stutter, momentarily at a loss for words. "Congratulations. I mean, I hope it's a good thing."

Jessica twists her lips. "It's a hot mess to be honest. Me and my boyfriend split recently."

"I'm sorry," I say, still struggling to absorb the news. A cold anger rises up inside me like a toxic mist. A pregnant dopehead. And Lynn West is facilitating her—endangering yet another baby's life.

"Yeah, me too." She pulls out a lip gloss and dabs at her lips.

"Is it a boy or a girl?"

"Dunno. I don't want to know."

I close the lid of my laptop and turn to her, a concerned expression on my face. "Are you going to keep the baby?"

She narrows her eyes at me. "Why do you ask?"

"No reason," I reply, my pulse throbbing in my throat. "Except it's bound to be more difficult as a single mother, trying to raise a child on your own and all."

Jessica smirks. "Don't worry, the baby's father will pay his fair share."

"Well, I'm glad you're going to make sure your ex supports his child. There's nothing worse than a deadbeat father."

Jessica gives me a funny look and gets to her feet. "I should probably get going. I told the Wests I'd be back for dinner tonight."

I put away my laptop and accompany her to the front door.

As she hurries down the steps and cuts across the lawn, my mind races to compute the implications of this new development. It might not be as easy to get rid of Jessica as I thought. I can't risk anything happening to her child. I'll have to delay executing my plan until after the baby is born.

10

_____

APRIL 17, 2008

I've been pacing the kitchen floor for hours, checking the baby monitor every two minutes to make sure Jonathan is still in his crib, safe and asleep. It's three in the morning and I know I won't be able to sleep tonight. My heart is still racing as I write this. I've had to white out several parts already because I keep messing up. Somehow this journal has turned into something that centers around you, like everything else in my life. My thoughts are a jumbled mess. I don't know if I'm coming or going. I packed a bag earlier. My things and Jonathan's. I was all set to leave you. I had Jonathan strapped into his car seat and everything, but then I had second thoughts.

I'm worried about how he'll feel waking up in the morning in a strange hotel room. I can't do that to him. I can't make any rash moves. I need to think this through. If I leave, when I leave, it has to be part of a well-thought-out plan with Jonathan's best interests at heart. I know one thing for sure, I'll never leave you alone with our son again.

You promised me you hadn't used in over two weeks, and you have been calmer in the past few days. We've actually been eating dinner together again. Like a real family. I believed you when you said you'd turned a corner. You knew I had to make an appearance at my boss's retirement party tonight. You said it would be good for you to spend some time alone with Jonathan. I wanted that too, for both your sakes. I trusted you. I only went to the party for an hour, but when I came back you were fast asleep on the couch, a prescription bottle wedged between the cushions. I found our two-year-old son wandering about in the back yard, filthy, alone, and unsupervised, apart from Bella, who was following him around like the faithful mutt she is.

I can't even describe the white-hot rage that flooded through me after the relief of finding him unhurt had subsided. I bathed him and put him to bed, then tried to shake you awake, but the only response was the sliver of drool trickling from your lips.

I wonder if I'll ever be able to sleep again. I can't even close my eyes without horrific images of what could have happened to Jonathan flooding my mind. Do you have any idea of the danger you put him in? What if he'd fallen into the fountain, or split his head open on a paver, or impaled himself on the garden rake leaning up against the wall? Anyone could have unlatched the gate and come around the side of the house and taken him. Even if a well-meaning neighbor had spotted him, they might have called child protective services on us if they'd discovered you high on the couch and me nowhere to be found. Jonathan could have been taken from us and placed in foster care. I can't let that happen. I won't let that happen. I will NEVER let anyone take Jonathan away!

11

PRESENT DAY

A few days later, Annie takes me to Ash Street to visit her friend Charles. His house boasts the most perfectly manicured lawn I have ever set eyes on, bordered by a precisely edged box hedge—every leaf the same glossy shade of green. The whole effect is so uniform it looks almost artificial. I can only imagine what kind of a time investment it takes to maintain his garden, not to mention the exorbitant cost of the organic fish fertilizer Annie says he uses. I'll need to be careful around Charles. Perfectionists have an annoying habit of noticing things that other people miss—like discrepancies in my story.

After ringing the doorbell repeatedly to no avail, Annie and I let ourselves in through the side gate. We find Charles pottering around at the bottom of his garden wielding a trowel and dodging the sun beneath a wide-brimmed hat.

"Morning ladies," he says, resting a gloved hand on the small of his back as he squints at us.

I make a fuss over Daisy, who barks and wags her tail in response, and then we take the obligatory tour of Charles' tomatoes. He hobbles up and down between the beds, talking

39

about the plants like they're his children, caressing their leaves and calling them by name. "Try one of these grape tomatoes," he urges, pulling one from its stalk and handing it to me. "They make a perfect mid-morning snack."

I pop one in my mouth, savoring the sweet, juicy taste that explodes when I bite through the crisp skin. "Yum! They really are excellent. Is gardening just a hobby or did you do this as a career?"

Charles smiles. "No, I'm a retired police officer."

The skin of the tomato sticks in my throat. My mouth is suddenly dry as sandpaper as I try not to choke. A prickling sensation works its way up my spine, all my senses on full alert. What if he remembers the news story and recognizes me? Or spots a hole in my fabricated resume, some incongruous detail police officers are trained to pick up on? I will myself to stay calm, reminding myself that he's an elderly retiree, more interested in vegetable plots than crime. Besides, I have a new name now and a totally different look. There's nothing to connect me to what happened.

"Over there I'm growing heirlooms," Charles continues, sparing me from having to piece together an appropriate response. He points at a towering trellis mantled with leafy plants, apparently oblivious to the turmoil he has unleashed in me. "I like a nice meaty heirloom on my burger every now and then. Better Boys and Early Girls are at the far end of the beds, and I put in a few Roma plants also." He winks at Annie. "I have a good friend who makes a great spaghetti sauce, and she's always kind enough to give me a batch for my freezer."

Annie chuckles and flaps a hand dismissively through the air. "I don't do much cooking these days."

After we've spent the best part of an hour wandering around the garden discussing the merits of each variety of tomato plant, and Charles has adjusted the drip irrigation system to his satisfaction, he invites us in for a coffee. I step into his kitchen and dart a wary glance around, half-afraid he might have a camera system rigged up somewhere. He could pull the footage later and use facial recognition software to find out who I am. It seems like something a retired police officer might do. On some level, I know I'm being ridiculous —paranoid Doctor Miller would say—but anxiety is writhing around in my gut like a serpent. I pinch the skin on the inside of my wrist trying to snap myself out of a familiar downward spiral.

Annie and I sit down at the kitchen table and make ourselves comfortable while Charles pulls off his gloves and proceeds to scrub his hands at the sink. "Are you settling into the neighborhood all right, Nora?" he inquires.

"Yes, thank you. Everyone is so friendly. Someone is always dropping off goodies—home-made cookies or fresh vegetables from their gardens."

"Sounds like I have some competition." Charles chortles as he lifts down three mugs from a wooden rack and sets them in front of an antiquated coffee maker. "I hope you drink coffee. I'm afraid that's pretty much all I've got."

I'd prefer to give caffeine a wide berth as my heart's still flapping around in my chest like a demented bat, but I can pass myself off with a few sips. "Coffee's fine, thank you."

Daisy trots over and looks up at me expectantly. I pick her up and cradle her in my lap, comforted by the warmth of her little body and her unconditional acceptance. Dogs don't judge like people do. They don't know or care how messed up you are on the inside. As long as you tickle their belly and rub their ears, you're good enough for them. "Daisy sure is a friendly girl. I miss not having a dog anymore."

"What kind of a dog did you have?" Annie asks.

"A little pug called Bella."

41

Annie offers a sympathetic smile. "Aw, that must have been hard to lose her. Those little dogs live a long time."

"She was only two years old when she died." The words slip from my lips before I think about what I'm saying.

"Oh, no!" Annie exclaims. "What happened to the poor little thing?"

"A car ... not far from my house ... " My voice trails off, my eyes pooling with tears. I shouldn't have brought it up. I can't give them any more details. They might connect me to that awful night.

Charles traces his fingers over his furrowed brow. "Dang drivers nowadays. The speed they drive through residential neighborhoods at is disgraceful."

I try to blot my tears with the back of my hand before they spill down my cheeks.

Annie leans over and pats me on the knee. "Don't blame yourself, dear. Dogs always manage to find a way to get out of the house or off the leash."

I drop my gaze and focus on petting Daisy. It didn't go down like they think. And losing Bella wasn't the worse part, not by a long shot. I don't blame myself for what happened. There are only two people to blame, and only one I can hold accountable.

Charles sips his coffee and peers over the rim of his mug at me. I shift uncomfortably under his scrutiny. I wonder if he can tell just by looking at a person if they're lying or hiding something.

"You can come by and pick up my Daisy any time you need some dog lovin'," he says, eliminating my unfounded fear that he's trying to recall where he knows me from. "Her legs may be short, but she sure loves going to the park for a walk. It's hard for me to take her anymore with the arthritis in my knee flaring up the way it does."

"Thanks," I choke out. "I'd like that."

Annie gathers up our mugs and sets them in the sink. "Well, we should be off. I have an appointment this afternoon. You wait, Nora. When you get to our age, your days will be filled with doctors' appointments—that and telemarketers. And somewhere in there you have to fit in a nap just to keep up."

Charles grunts his agreement. "Don't forget the gardening, although you don't do much of that, do you, Annie?"

She swats him with the tea towel she's holding. "Never was my thing. I do a much better job in the kitchen."

"That you do," Charles agrees.

I set Daisy down on the floor and get to my feet. "Thanks for the coffee and the tour of your garden, Charles. I'll come by and pick Daisy up for a walk one of these afternoons."

After all, I do love dogs. And a dog could prove very useful for the little shock-and-awe scenario I've dreamed up for Lynn West's benefit.

12

MAY 21, 2008

I really thought you were committed to getting better after the scare with Jonathan. The following morning, I sat you down at the kitchen table and told you that I'd found him in a soiled diaper playing with a broken terra-cotta pot in the back yard when I came back from the party. At first you tried to deny everything, but when I presented you with the empty prescription bottle and the photo I'd taken of you drooling on the couch, you actually showed some emotion and cried. Your remorse seemed genuine when you asked for one more chance. You agreed to go to therapy. I thought it was helping this past few weeks. I believed you when you said you'd quit for good this time.

Until yesterday, when I found our next-door neighbor's Ambien prescription in the glove box in your car. I'm not ashamed to say I've been keeping an eye on your old hiding places, just in case. You probably snuck into their bathroom and stole it when we were over for dinner last week. And of course when I confronted you about it, you went right back to your old ways, layering more lies on top of the ones you'd already fed me. You made up some lame story about Jill asking you to refill her husband's prescription. I didn't press *you on the issue, but we both know it doesn't make any sense. Jill works in town, only a few doors down from a pharmacy.*

Even so, I didn't want to believe you'd relapsed at first. I decided to sleep on it and call Jill the next day and ask her directly. I knew it would mean opening up about your addiction to the neighbors, something I was willing to do if that's what it took to get at the truth. But fate intervened. While you were in the shower this morning, a doctor's office called and left a message on your phone about an urgent prescription refill. It's not our usual doctor. It's proof positive that you're back to your old tricks. It sickens me to think that those wretched pills are more important to you than our marriage or our son.

I hate myself for being such a coward for so long—for lying to our friends and family, even keeping the truth from our neighbors. For covering up for you when you were inexplicably sick, or unavailable, or sleeping for longer and longer periods of time on the weekends. Most of all, I hate pretending to myself that this is temporary, that one day I'll wake up and you'll be clean, and this will all be a distant memory. Sometimes I think I'm going to explode with rage at you for what you're doing to yourself, to us, to our son. I can't remember the last time I laughed wholeheartedly at anything. Instead, I grimace and carry on as usual. But that's about to change. I'm making plans of my own.

13

PRESENT DAY

I've spent a lot of time over the past few weeks thinking about ways to persuade Jessica to move out. She hasn't told me anything useful about Lynn West that I don't already know, and she's in the way. I'm growing more anxious by the day, and I don't want to delay what I came here to do until after her baby's born.

The following Monday, I make a point of bumping into Jessica as she's walking home from the bus stop. "Hey, how was your day?"

She chews her gum and rolls her eyes. "It sucked."

I shoot her what I hope passes as a sincere look of empathy. "What happened?"

"Absolutely nothing. That's what. I'm bored sick helping out in that wretched canteen. I might as well be working in a soup kitchen. And I can't stand the smell anymore either. It's nauseating. I wish Rick would let me do some office work or something for him instead."

"What about taking classes?"

Jessica curls her lip in contempt. "I'm having a baby soon, remember? How am I supposed to show up for classes?" She lets out a dramatic sigh. "No, I just have to suffer through the next couple of months. Once the baby's born, I'll be free to go back to school, or set up my own business, like you did."

I digest this information as we walk in step. It doesn't sound as if she's planning on keeping the baby. She's been vague about it any time the topic comes up. Maybe she's decided to give it up for adoption after all. "Are you going to stay on with Rick and Lynn after the baby's born?"

Jessica throws me a look of disgust. "Are you kidding me? It's a total drag living there. Everyone thinks Rick and Lynn are so amazing, but they don't know the half of it. He's full of himself and she's a control freak."

A flicker of excitement darts through me. Finally a nugget of information I can work with. A crack in the perfect marriage. I tighten my brow in a concerned frown. "Are they treating you all right, Jessica?"

She blows out an exasperated breath. "Sort of, I guess. I mean they're death on me drinking or smoking, which I kinda get, but Lynn watches everything I eat, she even tries to tell me when I should go to bed. Ugh! I've had it up to here with the babysitting."

I make a soothing sound. "I'm sure she's only trying to look out for you and the baby."

"It's suffocating. She always thinks she knows what's best."

I press my nails into the palms of my hands. Lynn always did. If only Jessica knew just how questionable Lynn's judgement really is. The decisions she made ripped my world apart. And she's never been held accountable, yet. "You're always welcome to stay at my house if you need a break," I suggest.

Jessica's blue eyes latch onto me, a hawk-like suspicion in their gleam. "Why would you make an offer like that? You barely know me."

I grimace inwardly. I need to back off, tread with more

caution. Despite my efforts to connect, we're not best buddies. In actual fact, we're virtual strangers. I give a playful shrug of my shoulders. "I know where you live, and if you give me any trouble, I can always send you packing."

Jessica laughs, her expression relaxing. "I'll keep your offer in mind."

We part ways at the bottom of my driveway and I wave good-bye as she takes a shortcut over my lawn to her flat. I watch her open the side door and disappear inside. Maybe she'll reconsider my offer more seriously in the coming days. If I can't get her out of the Wests' house soon, I'll have to embark on a more drastic course of action.

I head inside my place, and open the kitchen window to let in some fresh air, before setting about making myself something to eat. I'm halfway through a roasted red pepper and chicken sandwich, enjoying the sound of the birds chirping in the evening sun, when raised voices drift my way from next door. I can tell they're female, and they sound as if they're arguing, but I've no idea what about. It must be Lynn and Jessica. I strain to make out the words, but to no avail. This could be worth listening in on. Abandoning my sandwich, I quietly open the back door and step out into my garden. I take a shallow breath and make my way toward the overgrown hedge that separates our yards.

"That wasn't part of the arrangement!" Lynn retorts.

"Exactly! I don't have to live where you tell me to live, or work where you tell me to work."

"You wouldn't even have a job if it wasn't for Rick." Lynn lowers her voice and her next words are lost to me.

I tiptoe closer along the hedge, a dappled shadow in and out of the rays of evening sun poking through the leaves.

"If it wasn't for Rick?" Jessica yells. "Are you for real? If it wasn't for Rick, I wouldn't be in this—"

The voices cut off abruptly. I hear a brief muffled

exchange before the patio door slams. I wonder if they spotted me and went inside to finish their argument. I wait another minute or two to make sure they don't come out to investigate, before heading back inside my house to finish my sandwich.

Moments later while I'm still trying to make sense of what I overheard, my doorbell rings. My insides churn with apprehension, the undigested food lying heavy in my stomach. I open the front door expecting to see Jessica with a duffle bag needing a place to spend the night, but instead, a pale-faced Lynn is standing on my doorstep, her brown hair scraped back from her face in an unflattering ponytail. Her smile is strained as she greets me.

"Hi Nora, I just ... wanted to apologize."

I raise my brows, my gut filled with misgivings. My heart thunders in my chest. Has she figured out who I am? "I don't follow. Apologize for what?"

She fiddles with the button on her shirt sleeve. "Can I come in for a minute?"

Reluctantly stepping back from the door, I motion for her to come inside. I lead her into the family room, still littered with moving boxes. I've been loath to unpack anything other than the bare necessities, but things are turning out to be more complicated than I anticipated. I've already been here for longer than I planned. I clear a space on the couch and wait until Lynn settles herself before asking coldly, "What did you want to apologize for?"

She blinks rapidly. "I saw you earlier in the garden. You must have heard us arguing." She arches a meaningful brow. "Jessica and I."

I wave a hand through the space between us. "I didn't pay much attention, to be honest. It can't be easy, your arrangement, having her living in the house with you." I clear my throat. "You know, with the hormones and all."

Lynn's eyes flash with anger but she quickly composes herself. "I take it she told you she's pregnant."

I give an apologetic nod. "I haven't mentioned it to anyone else if that's what you're getting at."

"I appreciate that," Lynn replies through gritted teeth. "It's a complicated situation."

"Of course. It was very generous of you and Rick to take her in after her boyfriend kicked her out. It would be understandable if you changed your mind. If it's any help at all, Jessica is welcome to stay with me until the baby's born."

I hold my breath, waiting on her response. For a moment, I think she's going to take me up on my offer, but then she lets out a weary sigh. "I can't say I blame him, the boyfriend I mean. You see, it's not his baby. It's ours, mine and Rick's."

I frown, trying to make sense of what she's saying but her words are spinning around in my head like wheels churning up mud and going nowhere.

Sensing my confusion, Lynn leans forward, an earnest look on her face. "Jessica's our surrogate."

14

MAY 29, 2008

oday was our wedding anniversary and you forgot all about it. You forgot all about the arbor beside the river where we pledged our lives to one another. And the horse and carriage that took us through the vineyard to our reception. And the triple chocolate fudge cake we fed each other and washed down with champagne. Four years we've been married, but it feels as if the last six months have erased everything we built in the previous three-and-a-half years together—everything except for Jonathan. He still brings me joy every day, and I'm so thankful he's in our lives. But today was supposed to have been about us. I pulled this journal out with every intention of writing about how lonely and hollow I feel inside, but my eyes are so blurry with tears, I can barely see the words on the page. I feel like I'm just punishing myself. It hurts to write about you. This isn't the first thing I penned with you in mind today. I left the anniversary card I picked out for you on your pillow, but you didn't even notice it slipping between the headboard and the mattress when you fell into bed all drugged up. I'm embarrassed to say that, in a fit of rage, I tossed it into the fire pit in the back yard and watched it burn.

Now that I've calmed down, I want to tell you that I still love you and wish I could hold you in my arms. I'll describe the card I got for you just in case one day you regret missing out on our fourth wedding anniversary. The truth is, I had a hard time choosing a card for you this year because so many of the messages don't fit us anymore—they're fictional, almost as full of lies as you are. Anyway, this particular card caught my eye because there was a couple zip-lining in the picture on the front. Remember when we went zip-lining over the waterfalls on our honeymoon? Probably not. Maybe you don't even remember where we went on our honeymoon. Costa Rica, The Laguna Resort, Room 505. You kept the card key. There was a time those kinds of things meant something to you.

Back to the anniversary card I barbecued...it was actually perfect for where we're at right now. The message inside read, "Love isn't a fairytale or a storybook. It's about overcoming obstacles and hanging on to each other. And every hour and minute is worth it because we do it together."

I still feel that way about us, but I'm not sure you do anymore. That's the hard part, accepting that you're willing to give up on us, on everything we hoped to become, for this addiction.

The tears are falling again. I can't stop this time. It's all so overwhelming. I'm going to close this journal for now and come back to it another day.

15

PRESENT DAY

*I*t's ours, mine and Rick's ... Jessica's our surrogate.

      I stare in horror at Lynn, bile surging up my throat. The audacity of her! How dare she dream of doing such a thing! She's not fit to be a mother. She doesn't deserve a child, not after taking my son from me. I wet my lips nervously, wracking my brains for something to say. She's dangerous, unhinged—Jessica's baby is at risk. I need to choose my next words wisely. I can't tip her off to the fact that I know who she is and what she's done. More importantly, I can't let her know who I am.

"We advertised on Craigslist," Lynn blurts out before I can say anything. "Jessica was one of several women who answered the ad. Rick recognized her from the youth program at the community center years ago. She'd just moved back to the area and needed the money." Lynn tinkles a laugh. "She's our silent partner so to speak."

"Oh," I say, sounding breathless. I'm still fending off the shock of Lynn becoming a mother, and worse, letting a dopehead carry her child. It's like she has no remorse. How can she even contemplate something like this after what she allowed to happen to my child? She might as well have pulled out a gun and shot him in the head. I will myself to stay calm, repeating the mantras in my head that Doctor Miller taught me.

"I'm only sharing this with you because you overheard us and I don't want you to misconstrue what was said," Lynn continues. "Unfortunately, I can't have children, but Rick and I both want them."

I give a tentative nod, not trusting myself to speak, but not entirely trusting what I'm hearing either. She seems overly eager to explain the situation to me. Why would she agree to a druggie carrying their child? Does she really think Jessica's clean nowadays? And why didn't Jessica tell me she was their surrogate? Something isn't adding up, but I can't put my finger on it. My head is swimming with confusion.

Lynn studies me for a moment. "You're not allergic to walnuts, are you?"

I frown, taken aback at the abrupt change in topic. "Walnuts? Uh, no."

"Good." She beams at me. "I'll pop around later with a walnut honey cake. I still owe you some fresh baked goodies. Lactose-free this time, I promise." She hesitates, picking at the skin around her fingers. "By the way, I'd rather you didn't tell anyone about our arrangement with Jessica, at least not until after the baby's born healthy and all the paperwork has been signed."

She stands and exits the room without waiting for my response. When the front door clicks shut behind her, I sink back in the couch and slide down, shaking all over. I can't let her have Jessica's baby. I can't let my enemy have what she took from me.

I drop my head into my hands, images of my son flashing before my eyes. Jonathan was born healthy. But it doesn't matter if babies are born healthy because sometimes, they die anyway. As Lynn knows only too well.

I DIDN'T SLEEP MUCH last night. And when I did, I dreamed of Jonathan. So handsome, so perfectly formed, so full of potential. Until she took it all away. My brain is fogged with fatigue this morning, but the important thing is that I have a new plan. It's not the plan I came here with—to destroy Lynn West and avenge my son. That plan had to be shelved, temporarily. The priority now is to save Jessica's baby. It's evident Jessica doesn't care what becomes of him if she's willing to hand him over to someone like Lynn. And Lynn doesn't care either—she's willing to let a dopehead give birth to her child. So, I must become his advocate. I know he's a boy. I can sense it, just like I knew Jonathan was a boy long before the ultrasound confirmed it. I never doubted my instincts then, and I trust them now. Saving this baby is the right thing to do.

It will be harder than ever to cover my tracks going forward. I have to make Jessica and her baby disappear under suspicious circumstances, and make sure Rick and Lynn take the fall. It's poetic justice, in a sense. I can have it all—their baby, their marriage, and revenge. It's just a matter of laying the groundwork beforehand and introducing enough doubt about their character. I'm good at sowing discord. Doctor Miller told me that in one of our therapy sessions. And although it hurt at the time, I have to admit it's true. If I hadn't been estranged from my husband, Jonathan and Bella might not have died that night. But I wasn't there to protect them, thanks to Lynn's meddling.

I watch for Jessica walking home from the bus stop and make a point of going out to my mailbox right before she passes my driveway. "Hey, I got some new stock in for my website if you want to take a look," I say, leafing through the envelopes in my hand.

"What's the point?" Jessica groans. "Nothing will fit for much longer. I already feel fat."

"You can still try stuff on. That way you'll have something to wear after the baby's born."

Jessica shrugs, one thumb jammed firmly in the shoulder strap of her backpack. "Whatever."

She follows me inside and I take her straight through to the family room where I've laid out some articles of clothing that I selected with her in mind. Sure enough, her eyes light up as she begins rifling through the items. "These are pretty cool."

"Why don't you try a few on? Take whatever you want into the bathroom."

Jessica wastes no time selecting several pieces and disappears with them. When she comes back a few minutes later, her face is flushed but she's grinning from ear to ear. "I like these," she simpers, holding up a long-sleeved sweater and a blouse.

"Then they're yours," I say. "I got some free samples, so they didn't cost me a thing."

"Are you sure?" Jessica clutches the clothes to her chest. "I mean, these tops are really cool."

"Absolutely," I reply, getting to my feet. "Do you want a soda or something?"

She twists her lips. "I'd kill for a Coke. Lynn won't even let me drink soda anymore."

I return with two Cokes and hand one to her, my iPhone set to record in my pocket. The first phase of my plan involves gathering evidence that Jessica is being mistreated —or in this case, evidence I can doctor later. I just need to make sure to insert all the right terms into our conversation. "So, I take it Lynn and Rick are still acting like overbearing parents?" I ask, sinking down next to her on the couch.

"Ugh, I feel like a prisoner sometimes," Jessica says in her usual dramatic fashion. She takes a swig of soda and flops back against the throw pillows. "Rick even makes a point of locking the doors when I come home in the evening. They don't want me going out anywhere at night, partying or whatever."

I give a hollow laugh. "At least they don't lock you in your flat." I quickly paint a concerned expression on my face. "They don't, do they? I mean that would be a form of abuse. Are they abusing you? You're not afraid of them or anything, are you?"

"Afraid? No, of course not," she scoffs. "They're super annoying, that's all."

I twist my hands in my lap and glance across at her again. "I suppose it's understandable that they're concerned." I hesitate before adding, "Lynn told me everything."

Jessica stiffens, then scrambles to sit upright in the couch, almost dropping her Coke in the process. "What do you mean? What did she tell you?"

"You know, about your hush-hush surrogacy—the whole silent partner thing," I lower my voice to a respectful whisper.

Jessica's face clears. "Oh, that. I ... didn't realize they were telling people already."

"They're not, at least they weren't. I kind of overheard you and Lynn arguing yesterday and she wanted to set the record straight."

Jessica gives a hesitant nod, avoiding my gaze. "Yeah, I answered an ad they put on Craigslist. Once Rick realized he knew me from the youth program, he and Lynn decided I would be a good match."

It's almost word-for-word what Lynn said. As if they'd

rehearsed it. I'm more convinced than ever that I'm not getting the whole story. We sit in silence for a moment or two before I ask, "Why did you want to become their surrogate?"

Jessica picks at the ring on her can. "Rick helped me out a lot over the years. I wanted to return the favor."

I stare at her, unconvinced. "Is that what they told you to say?"

Jessica sighs. "Okay, I admit, it wasn't just a good deed. I needed the money. I lost my job, and when my boyfriend kicked me out ... well, it seemed like a good opportunity. They were offering ten thousand dollars." She fingers the piercing above her left eyebrow. "You don't judge me for renting out my womb, do you?"

I struggle to keep a deadpan expression. Of course, I judge her, but not for becoming a surrogate. I judge her for being a liar. Annie's words have been echoing in my ear for days now, and finally, it all makes sense.

Jessica's acting very cagey about the whole episode, if you ask me.

The Wests are not paying her to be their surrogate, they're paying her to keep her mouth shut. I almost feel sorry for Lynn. She's made another bad judgement call, but she should know by now that druggies can never really be trusted. Evidently, Slick Rick had second thoughts about marrying his savior. I think I can guess what he's been up to, and what Lynn's trying to cover up.

16

he mail truck came a few minutes ago and I watched through the family room window as you hurried out to the mailbox to retrieve the package containing your latest prescription. Do you really think I don't know what you're doing? You were furious when I called your local doctor and cut off your supply, so I know the last thing you want is for me to find out about your recurring mail order. I have to admit you're very resourceful when it comes to finding ways to keep an endless supply of Adderall on hand—and sleeping pills as downers. But I've seen the charges from online pharmacies on your credit card bill. You've never shared your log in credentials with me, but I can be resourceful too.

What you don't realize is that people are beginning to pick up on things. You think the drugs don't affect you, but they do. They make you more aggressive and paranoid. You've lost weight recently too, and it doesn't suit you. You're fobbing everyone off by telling them your job is particularly stressful these days. But you don't notice how their eyes flick to me for confirmation. There was a time I would have gone along with the sham, but now I just look away. I figure that tells them all they need to know.

You're still holding down your job, for now at least. But at home you're spending more and more time on your own, getting high or sleeping off the effects of your latest fix. Your Adderall hours take priority over the rest of your life. Only last week, I found some white powder on the edge of the bathroom sink. I suspect you've started crushing your pills and snorting them. I know you get high faster that way. A lethal practice that can trigger heart attacks or strokes. I don't want our son to be here when that happens. What you're doing is just another form of Russian roulette. And the irony is—you're the one who didn't want us to have a gun in the house with a toddler.

On the rare occasions when we are together in the evenings, you're always fidgety and irritable. Lately the depths of your rage scare me. You rarely play with Jonathan anymore, and in light of your recent mood swings, it's probably better that way. We're losing you to the drugs, and there's nothing I can do about it as long as you refuse to seek help.

I've been thinking about what to do. I've wrestled with all sorts of options, and I'm finally at peace with my decision. I'm going to give you an ultimatum. You have until the end of the summer to get clean or I'll leave and take our son with me.

17

PRESENT DAY

I called Annie and told her about Jessica's pregnancy before Lynn had a chance to, knowing it would be just the kind of juicy gossip that would secure Annie's loyalty and make her a useful ally for what I have in mind next. I didn't mention the surrogacy to her. As far as Annie knows, the ex-boyfriend is the father. I'm meeting her at a coffee shop today because I need to talk to her in person and start planting some seeds that paint Rick and Lynn in an unfavorable light. I didn't want to stop by her house and risk another close encounter with her fur fiend, Leo, and I couldn't invite her to my house either in case Jessica walked in on us.

I arrive at the coffee shop early and select an end table for two on the back wall where we'll have some privacy. Annie arrives punctually, as older people tend to do, and squints around the tables looking for me. I get to my feet and wave in an exaggerated fashion. Relief floods her features as she ambles over to greet me. "I thought for a moment I had mixed up where we were supposed to meet. I've never been

N. L. HINKENS

to this place before and I couldn't remember what you said it was called."

I flash her a charitable smile. "Steamed Beans."

"Such strange names they have for businesses nowadays." She darts a curious glance around. "This is one of those fancy coffee places where I never know what to order. When I was your age, we didn't have a menu for coffee. Coffee was coffee, and the only twist was with cream and sugar or without." She chuckles to herself as she unwinds her hand knit scarf and slips her arms out of her coat.

"In that case, how about I surprise you, something flavored, perhaps?" I suggest.

"No surprises for me," Annie says, sinking down in a chair. "Just a black coffee, please."

At the counter, I order a chai tea and a black coffee as well as a dairy-free bran muffin and a Danish pastry. After making a point of pretending to be lactose intolerant, I've been careful to stick to my script. I carry our drinks carefully back to our table, with a pastry balanced atop each. "How about a Danish pastry to go with your coffee?" I say, setting the cups down. "The muffin's dairy free. I can't do lactose, as you know."

"Thank you, dear. The Danish looks delicious."

I hand it to her and sit down opposite her at the table.

Annie removes the lid from her coffee and blows on it. "I still can't believe that Jessica's pregnant. She's not even showing yet—flat as a pancake. I was a whale when I was pregnant with my Timmy." She takes a bite of her cheese Danish and chews it thoughtfully. "I told you Jessica was acting very suspiciously. I bet that's why her boyfriend kicked her out in the first place." She lets out a humph. "It's not right, is it? I mean, if it wasn't for Rick and Lynn, she'd be sleeping in her car right about now."

I chew on my lip and frown at my tea for a moment. "Actually, Annie, I wanted to talk to you about that."

She washes down another mouthful of flaky pastry with a hasty gulp of coffee. "Go on."

"It's just that … well I'm not exactly sure how to say this, but I'm worried about Jessica."

"Jessica? Why?" Annie's brow folds into paper thin creases. "Is everything all right with the baby?"

"Yes, the baby's fine, as far as I know. But Jessica is unhappy."

Annie blinks across at me, considering this. "Well, I imagine she is to some extent. She's going to be a single mother. Her boyfriend wants nothing to do with her or the baby. It's probably not the way she envisioned things turning out at this stage of her life."

I shake my head. "It's not that. I mean she's unhappy living with Rick and Lynn.

Annie takes another sip of coffee, and frowns. "Well, I think it was more than generous of them to take her in and give her a roof over her head. She's a lucky girl, if you ask me, considering what a troublemaker she's been in the past."

I twirl my half-empty paper cup between my fingers. "I'm not convinced they did it out of the goodness of their hearts."

Annie stares at me, clearly confused. "I don't understand. What are you trying to say?"

I throw a furtive glance at the couple sitting down at the next table and then lean closer to Annie. "It's like they've got some kind of control over Jessica. I think they're hiding something. I don't know what it is exactly, but something seems off about this whole situation."

Annie's eyes widen. "Well I do love a good mystery, but I'm not sure I detect one here. Jessica's boyfriend kicked her out when he found out she was pregnant, and Rick and Lynn took her in. There's bound to be some tension from time to time. Jessica always did have a rebellious streak—all that drinking and drugs and carrying on when she was younger."

I grimace inwardly. I need to do better. Annie's still bent on championing Rick and Lynn as heroes. It's time to turn up the heat. "The truth is, Annie, Jessica feels like a prisoner there. They're forcing her to work at the community center in exchange for room and board. She's not a volunteer."

Annie's hand hovers in midair, a piece of cheese Danish inches from her mouth. She sets it back down on the plate and scratches her forehead. "Are you sure about that? Don't you think Jessica could be embellishing things?"

I shake my head. "No, I overheard Lynn and Jessica arguing yesterday. Lynn was yelling at her that she couldn't expect free room and board—she needed to earn her keep. Jessica even told me they lock the doors in the evening when she comes home so she can't go out anywhere. That's not normal."

Annie blinks, looking decidedly alarmed. "No, it certainly isn't. And I didn't realize they were making Jessica work to earn her keep. I assumed she had offered to help out at the community center."

I let out a heavy sigh. "Jessica's considering moving out before things get any worse. I said she could stay with me until the baby is born, but she thinks that would be too awkward for everyone. She wants to move out of state—she says she has friends in Indiana who will take her in."

Annie digests this information as she sips her coffee. "Well, I suppose that might not be a bad idea if things aren't going to work out here."

I nod. "You won't say anything to anyone, will you? Jessica told me all this in confidence, and I don't want to start any rumors that will make things worse for her than they already are. It's just that I needed to bounce it off someone. After all,

I'm new to the neighborhood, and it's rather upsetting to have all this going on next door."

Annie reaches across the table and pats my hand. "You did the right thing coming to me, dear. It does sound as if the Wests are taking advantage of Jessica. Rick comes across as such a charmer, but like I always said, he's a little too smooth for his own good. He'd better not be taking advantage of those kids he puts through the youth programs. You don't mind if I run this by Charles and see what he thinks, do you? Being a retired police officer, he has a lot of insight into these kinds of situations. He'll keep it in the strictest confidence, of course."

I give a small shrug. "I suppose it can't do any harm. I've been so worried about Jessica—I'm glad she confided in me about what's going on. At least now if she disappears, we'll know why."

....

18

JULY 08, 2008

*A*ll your deception and never-ending lies have been driving
me crazy. Somehow everything keeps getting twisted
around until it's all my fault and I find myself questioning my
reasons for leaving you. Am I really justified in taking Jonathan
away from you? It's a life-changing decision and I don't take it
lightly. I found a local support group a couple of weeks back and
I've secretly been attending their meetings. I guess I wanted
someone who's farther along in this journey to reassure me that I'm
on the right path.

The first time I pulled into the church parking lot where the
group meets, I almost bailed. I sat in the car with my head on the
steering wheel until a man knocked on my window. "First time's
the worst," he said. "I'll walk you in."

I can't tell you how much it meant to open up to people who
understood. It's a huge relief to talk to other spouses who know
exactly what it's like living with someone who manipulates every
word you say and manages to convince you they didn't do what you
know they did—that you simply misunderstood or overreacted. The
group confirmed a lot of things for me, including the legitimacy of
my ultimatum. So I'm going to stick by my deadline and not extend

it, even though you've asked me to and told me I'm harsh and uncaring for not giving you the time you need.

The group also told me not to put any more energy or time into your recovery. Apparently, I'm an enabler, addicted to addiction so to speak. Who would have thought that's even a thing? I admit it is oddly comforting in its familiarity in an uncomfortable sort of way. In contrast, the thought of starting over without you is terrifying and alien. But I see what they're saying, and I need to break free of this web you have me tangled up in. They also said it's time I started taking better care of myself. I've been feeling rundown lately, but it feels so indulgent to think about me at a time like this. All I ever wanted was to take care of you and Jonathan. But you won't let me.

One of the most important things I've had to accept is that it's a waste of time trying to guilt you into quitting. The compulsion to get high is too strong. So I've stopped listing off all the ways you've hurt me and all the times you've lied to me about where you were going when you were actually picking up prescriptions—even buying prescription drugs illegally on the street. Oh yes, I know all about your treks to the seedy part of town. I put a tracking app on your phone. As cold as it sounds, I need hard evidence for a potential custody case down the line.

Now that I've admitted to myself that I've been an enabler, I'm going to have to change a few of my own behaviors. I need to quit researching the topic for starters. I can't keep Googling late at night about ways to help you, hoping to find some new tidbit of information that might save you. It's too late for that. All I can do now is focus my efforts on saving Jonathan.

19

PRESENT DAY

I've started picking up Daisy three afternoons a week and taking her on a walk to the park. In return, Charles keeps me well stocked with tomatoes. More important, he's taking my concerns about the alleged abuse going on next door seriously. He's asked me to document everything. I've gone one step further and instructed Jessica to write it all down in a diary of sorts, which she keeps on her laptop. I even encouraged her to embellish it, to think of it as insurance in case the Wests ever find out she's smoking weed and try to renege on the ten-thousand dollars. The look of horror on Jessica's face when she realized I knew all about her secret habit was priceless. She has been putty in my hands ever since. The diary is insurance, in a way, but, unbeknownst to Jessica, I'm the beneficiary. It's another piece of evidence to add to the growing collection that will ultimately serve to shatter my enemy's life.

I let myself into Charles' backyard through the latticed side gate, which doesn't creak thanks to the rigorous maintenance schedule he keeps track of on a color-coded spreadsheet. He's meticulous about everything, which is why I'm being equally vigilant about the information I share with him, making sure I don't contradict myself at any point along the way. I smile when Daisy comes trotting up to greet me, her little tail wagging with enthusiasm. So far everything is going according to plan. Even Daisy's sensitive nose hasn't been able to sniff out my subterfuge.

"Afternoon, Nora," Charles calls out, waving a clay-caked glove in my direction. He's kneeling on some sort of rubber-ized pad, tying up wayward tendrils on his tomato plants.

"You're hard at it again, Charles."

"Almost done here, trying to wrap things up and get out of the sun."

I kneel and make a fuss over Daisy before heading inside the house to fetch her leash hanging on the coat rack next to the back door. Charles always tells me to make myself at home and take a bottle of water from the fridge for my walk —he even showed me where he keeps his spare key for the days he is off visiting his grandkids and needs me to walk Daisy. He's surprisingly trusting for a retired police officer, which makes me think I've done a good job of blending into the community. In a few short months, I've managed to build his trust, just like I've built the trust of the other key people I'll need to execute my plan.

"See you later!" I say with a quick wave in his direction.

"Thanks, Nora. Take your time. I might lie down for a nap in a bit. This heat has flat worn me out today."

Daisy and I set off toward the park, the sun glaring down on us like an angry celestial eye. I wonder if it can see through to my soul, if it knows I am bent on retribution. It can do nothing to stop me, other than beat down on me. I'll be drenched in sweat by the time Daisy and I get back, but it feels good to be out in the fresh air and getting regular exer-cise again. For too many months, I lay curled up in a ball wishing away the pain inside me. Doctor Miller was wrong to think it would get better with time. Instead, it only fermented, draining the energy from me until I scarcely had the will to live some days. Revenge has given me a renewed purpose.

Daisy is as well-trained as one would expect of any dog belonging to Charles. She walks to heel, doing a good job of keeping up with me despite her short legs. We have managed to form a tight bond in a short time. I know she won't let me down when the time comes for her little performance. When we reach the park, I slow the pace and let her sniff around her favorite bushes for interesting new smells. After she has satisfied her curiosity, I sit down on a nearby bench and pull out my water bottle.

A young woman approaches with a puppy on a leash. I suck in a sudden breath at the wave of pain that assaults me. It's a pug, only a few months old, the exact same coloring as Bella. My heart begins to thud ominously in my chest as the woman draws closer. I try not to stare, but my gaze is locked on the puppy—Bella's double. Tears well up inside me like a saltwater dam about to burst as memories of Jonathan and Bella force their way into my mind. I blink furiously and will myself to look away, but my eyes are quickly drawn back. The pug's attention is fixed on Daisy, its little curled tail wiggling to and fro in expectation of a frolic in the grass with a newfound friend.

"Beatrix! Come here, baby!" The young woman tugs gently on the leash. Ignoring the command, the puppy strains to run toward Daisy. The woman smiles across at me. "Is it all right if Beatrix greets your dog?"

No, no it isn't all right. It's all wrong. My heart's about to explode with pain. I'm sweating profusely, on the verge of bursting into tears, awash with harrowing flashbacks. "She's not mine," I manage with a wobble in my voice. "I'm not sure how she'll react to a puppy."

Undeterred by my ambiguous response, the woman ambles toward me. "I'm sure they'll be fine. I promise I won't let Beatrix get too frisky. She's very friendly."

Daisy does nothing to support me. Her tongue hangs out, displaying her excitement for all to see. The closer Beatrix gets, the faster Daisy's tail wags in anticipation.

To my horror, the woman sits down on the bench next to me. The two dogs greet each other exuberantly and immediately begin chasing each other around in circles. I sniff back my tears, reminding myself that the woman can't see my watery eyes behind my shades.

"What's the dog's name?" she asks.

I clear my throat before answering, "Daisy." I hurriedly screw the lid back on my water bottle and get to my feet. "Not to be rude or anything, but I really need to get her back to her owner. He's elderly and he worries if we're even a minute late."

The woman jumps up with an apologetic grimace. "No worries, I should get going too. Have a great rest of your day." She swoops up her puppy and strides off in the direction of the parking lot. Once she's out of sight, I sink back down on the bench and drop my head into my hands. Hot tears slide down my cheeks as shards of broken memories explode in my heart. Jonathan squealing excitedly, hands outstretched for Bella, and then those same pudgy hands folded reverently over his chest as he lay still and unmoving in his tiny white coffin.

So much for all those long months of therapy. Nothing has healed inside me. My brokenness has morphed into a raging monster that will only be sated by revenge.

JULY 24, 2008

I don't want to go to group therapy tonight. I'm tempted to call them up and tell them I'm never coming back. If I don't go, I can still pretend this isn't happening. I feel so lost and alone most days. Sometimes it's hard to envision a future where I'll ever be happy and carefree again. I'm so tired of everything in my life revolving around you and your destructive choices. Some of the things I hear at group scare me half to death. Last week one of the members shared her story of how she found out her husband of ten years was addicted to opioids. She was clueless until one day out of the blue she got a call at work from her neighbor telling her that the police were at her house and she was being evicted. She left work, stunned and confused, desperately trying to call her husband as she drove home. When she arrived at her house, strangers were hauling out her belongings and piling them up on the curb, randomly tossing smaller items into her baby's crib. She cried and pleaded with them to stop, insisting there must be some mistake, and that's when the police informed her that they'd posted multiple eviction notices Apparently, her husband hadn't been making the mortgage payments for months. Instead he'd been using the money to fund his drug addiction. He was so devious he even managed to intercept the eviction notices and mail, so his wife never knew a thing until the day she and her three kids were made homeless. Her husband skipped town and has never made a single child support payment.

I suppose you could say I'm lucky I found out before you destroyed everything we have. I can't imagine being blindsided like that poor woman, forced to watch her entire world crumble around her in an instant. The worst stories of course are always the ones where a loved one dies. I can't bear to look at the faces of the mothers and fathers in our group who've buried their kids. There's something so unnatural about laying your own child to rest that it seems to physically engrave itself on a parent's face.

When I shared some of these stories with you over dinner one night, you shook your head and said I was being melodramatic. "This isn't an addiction. I can stop whenever I want," you snapped. "Stop obsessing. We're not going to lose our house. I have a good job and I'm entitled to spend my money however I want."

Just a few minutes ago, you texted me that you're working late again. I know you're going to pay a visit to the wrong side of town. The "working late" thing is becoming more frequent, so I guess it's getting harder to keep up your supply through bogus prescriptions.

I can still make group in time if I leave now. I need to hear the voice of reason to counteract your crazy-making. I already have our neighbor lined up to babysit. I should probably go. I'm always glad when I do.

21

PRESENT DAY

I've taken over driving Jessica to her prenatal appointments. It was difficult for Lynn to keep taking time off work to do it, and she's grateful for the reprieve. Things have grown increasingly tense between her and Jessica. Jessica even spent the night at my place on a couple of occasions after a particularly feisty row. Hardly surprising considering they're both in love with the same man. But it's been a little disconcerting, at times, watching my enemy grow ever more dependent on me as the months go by. Because Lynn West is still my enemy—she destroyed my life, she's the reason Johnathan is dead.

Ancient wisdom requires a life for life. Why should I show Lynn West any mercy? She rescues strays who don't deserve to be rescued. Liars like my estranged husband and Rick. She's covering for what he did to Jessica, which makes her equally as despicable as him. Maybe she doesn't have any idea of the devastation her reckless decisions leave in their wake. But she'll know soon enough what it feels like to have her heart ripped out. After I've taken her husband's child and destroyed her marriage, I'll finish what I came here to do.

Today, Jessica and I are on our way to her thirty-six-week checkup. It's hard to believe she's this far along already. Annie thinks I'm a saint for watching out for Jessica. She's worried sick about her wellbeing after everything I've shared about what's been going on. I've been encouraging Jessica to drop a few hints directly to Annie about how controlling Lynn and Rick are behind closed doors. "It's a good idea to have more than one witness to their behavior in case the surrogacy arrangement falls through," I reminded Jessica yesterday. "After all, you don't have anything in writing, and you might find you need some leverage to get your money from Rick and Lynn at the end of the day."

Turns out, like every other druggie, Jessica's perfectly happy to play along when there's money at stake. I let her know that I'm on to her weed habit, and she was extremely thankful that I was willing to keep my mouth shut about it. She doesn't want to jeopardize her payout. On the whole, I've groomed her well. She's practically eating out of my hand at this point.

I edited the recording I made of her on my phone to make it sound as if she's afraid of the Wests—as though they've been holding her prisoner in their home. One important piece of the puzzle remains, but I'm going to hold off telling Jessica that I know the truth about her affair with Rick until I'm ready to make her disappear.

"I hope this baby comes soon," Jessica groans, adjusting her position in the passenger seat of my Nissan. The seatbelt is pulled down low around her belly and she holds it away from her body. "Everything is so uncomfortable."

"Yeah, it's hard at the end," I say, my eyes trained on the heavy traffic.

Jessica turns to me and arches a brow. "Wait, you've been pregnant?"

The back of my neck prickles with sweat as I calculate

how best to backtrack. That was incredibly careless of me. "Huh? Oh, sorry, I meant to say, I suppose it is. Gosh, I've never seen the traffic like this before. What on earth is going on?"

"Roadwork." Jessica yawns loudly. "Rick said something about it at breakfast."

"I wish I'd known," I reply, trying to curb the reprimand in my tone. "We could have left earlier."

"I couldn't possibly have gotten out of bed any earlier than I did," Jessica moans. "I'm so tired all the time."

We finally make it to the doctor's office but we're fifteen minutes late for the appointment and end up having to wait for almost a full hour before Doctor Barker manages to squeeze us in between patients. Jessica has asked me to be her labor coach, so I've been going to the appointments with her, pretending all of this is a fascinating new experience for me. Of course, the truth is that I know exactly what it's like to harbor a life in my womb. I wish Jonathan was still inside me. It was the only place I could ever really keep him safe.

I watch as Doctor Barker squeezes some gel onto Jessica's belly and then reaches for the ultrasound wand. Sadness seeps through me like a slow-working poison. I remember it like it was yesterday, watching the screen from Jessica's vantage point—lying on my back with my swollen belly rising like a mountain in front of me while my obstetrician took measurements and pointed out Jonathan's perfectly formed limbs, his tiny half-moon fingernails, the sturdy rhythm of his beating heart. Lynn took all of that away from me in one fateful ruling—a modern-day Caesar with her imperial thumbs down to my desperate request for custody.

"Well, the good news is that your baby's presenting head down," Doctor Barker says after completing her examination of Jessica. "The ideal starting position for labor. Are you sleeping okay?"

"Ugh, no. It's impossible to get comfortable."

Doctor Barker nods sympathetically. "Have you felt any contractions yet?"

Jessica pulls down the corners of her lips. "I wish. If there's anything I can do to help this baby along, I'm willing to give it a go."

"Babies come when they're ready—they know what they're doing. Your little one's heartbeat is great, and the growth rate is spot on." The doctor glances across at me. "Will you be at the birth?"

I nod. "Yes, I'm Jessica's birth partner."

Doctor Barker purses her lips and scribbles something in her notes. I don't think she approves. She probably thinks Lynn and Rick should be here instead of me. "Best be on standby from here on out. It's anybody's guess when the little one will make an appearance."

"I'm ready," I reply, giving Jessica a reassuring smile. "I live right next door, so I can be there in minutes."

Doctor Barker gets to her feet and pats Jessica on the arm. "Make another appointment for next week and don't be afraid to call in the meantime if you have any unusual symptoms—spotting, swelling, anything at all like that."

I help Jessica into a sitting position, and she slides awkwardly from the table and lumbers across the floor.

The doctor's hawk-eyed gaze homes in on me as I open the door. When she catches me staring back, she diverts her attention to the paperwork on her desk. I know she's wondering about the nature of my relationship with Jessica. After all, I'm not a relative, and I showed up halfway through her pregnancy. But Doctor Barker can wonder all she wants. I'm not the criminal here. Lynn West won't get away with taking another baby away from me. This time I intend to come out the winner.

AUGUST 09, 2008

It's time to begin envisioning a future without you. In fact, I've already begun. I have a vision board hidden in the garden shed. Someone at group suggested making one. I admit I dismissed it as one of those goofy, New Age ideas at first, but then I got to thinking about how it might be a good visual aid to help me explain things to Jonathan once he's old enough to start asking questions. I've pinned several pictures on the board of all the things I still want to do in life. Like see the Northern Lights and walk across the Great Wall of China. Remember how we talked about taking those trips together? Well I'm not going to stop living just because you've given up on us. I never wanted a future without you in it, but that's what it's come down to. Our white wedding has been reduced to a pile of gray ash. But I can build new dreams out of those ashes.

I've been following a blog for family members of addicts, and one of the things that stuck with me is that I'm still in charge of my own happiness, even though I can't control yours. You've cut me out of your life, so now I'm cutting a new life out of magazines for myself. Yesterday, I gave myself a paper cut in the process and bled all over the page, but the pain was nothing to the pain I feel inside.

You were in all my dreams of our future, so I've had to start from scratch with this vision board. I still don't know who I am without you. The truth is, I don't know what I want from my future or how exactly to begin this process. It's one thing making a bucket list and cutting and pasting catchy quotes on a piece of plywood, but it's another thing facing the day-to-day reality of living the next chapter of my life without you. I don't know what will make me happy, because I thought I had everything I ever wanted in you and Jonathan.

Anyway, back to the board. I'm not much of an artist so it's not something I'll ever hang up on a wall, but it's functional—it's helping me clarify what's really important. It's not an easy process to start dreaming again. But I've started taking small steps in the direction I want to go. I've put my favorite picture of Jonathan at the center. Having him there reminds me of what I have to be grateful for. You'll probably never set eyes on this board, but one day I'll show it to our son in the hope that it helps him heal. I want him to be strong. He needs to know to never give up, that life is always worth living even if there are days you have to fight for a future.

23

PRESENT DAY

*I*t's time to turn up the heat on the Wests. Once Jessica disappears, the police will need proof of a connection between her and Rick that goes beyond a surrogacy—incriminating evidence they were lovers—before they will agree to investigate. After thinking it through, I've decided to plant a card from Jessica in Rick's office. It has to be something that will hold up under scrutiny, so I can't forge her signature in case the police enlist a handwriting expert to examine it. It actually has to be Jessica's.

I've invited her to pop around this morning to check out a new collection of purses which, to all intents and purposes, I ordered for my online store. I told her she could pick one out for herself. It seems gifts are Jessica's love language, a fact I intend to put to good use when it comes time for her to disappear. I don't envision it being much of a problem talking her into the role I've planned for her to play once her baby is born.

Shortly before noon, I spot her waddling up to my front door. For someone who was scarcely showing until halfway through her pregnancy, she has managed to balloon in the last trimester. I fling open the door before she has a chance to ring the doorbell. "Come on in. You're gonna love what they've sent me."

I lead her into the family room where I've laid out some of the purses that I thought might catch her eye. The remainder are still wrapped in plastic in the box on the floor next to the couch, ready to be returned once Jessica has made her selection.

Eyes aglow, she immediately starts rifling through the options. "No way!" she exclaims, reaching for a studded black purse with an iron moon clasp. "This one's totally me." She peers inside it to examine the pockets, and then slips the strap over her shoulder and walks out to the hall to admire it in the mirror.

I watch as she pivots this way and that, the purse dangling at her side. From this profile, her belly looks enormous. I've seen the fried food she consumes when she's not under Lynn's watchful eye—her voracious appetite driven by her weed habit—and she's certainly not doing herself any favors. Or her baby. I clench my hands into fists at my sides and close my eyes briefly, willing myself to refocus. There's only so much I can control. Only so much I can do to keep this baby safe before it's born. It will all be so much easier when Jessica's out of the picture and he's with me.

I take a few deep breaths and then reach for the open card on the coffee table that I need Jessica to sign. Ostensibly, it's a birthday card for Annie, but what Jessica won't realize is that I've used some double-sided tape to attach a picture of a choir of fluffy cats singing "Happy Birthday" on top of a very sexy "Miss You Hot Stuff!" card.

"Can I have this one?" Jessica asks, bouncing back into the room, one thumb hooked through the strap of the black purse which caught her eye.

"Absolutely!" I beam at her. "Good choice. It suits you."

"Thanks, Nora. You're the best." She gathers up the remainder of the purses and lays them on top of the unopened ones in the box. "I should get going. I told Lynn I'd eat dinner with them tonight."

"Oh, real quick before you go. Can you sign this card for Annie? It's her birthday next week. I got her a cat card, of course. You know how crazy she is about Leo." I pick it up and flash the cover at Jessica briefly before laying it back down on the table. I casually hand her a pen while holding the card open. "That purse is totally you."

"I love it," Jessica enthuses, carelessly scribbling her name, one eye roving over the purse hanging from her shoulder. She tosses the pen on the coffee table. "I owe you one."

"No, you don't," I assure her, getting to my feet to escort her out. "You deserve to have a treat for yourself now and again. After all, what you're doing is so unselfish—being a surrogate and all."

A tiny frown flickers across her brow. "I feel so bad for people who can't have kids. It must be heartbreaking for them."

Liar! My nails dig into my palms. I want to scream at her and claw at her big blue eyes that are anything but innocent. How about people who lose their kids, Jessica? Do you feel bad for them too? Because that's worse than not having kids at all. It's me you should be feeling sorry for, not my enemy. I bite down on my lips hard and the metallic taste of blood floods my tongue. Lynn West will know what it feels like to have her world implode soon enough. I just need to keep my mouth shut and bide my time.

24

SEPTEMBER 19, 2008

*J*onathan's running a fever. I gave him some Tylenol
and he finally fell asleep. But I'm worried about him.
I don't want to go to bed in case he wakes up again. It
would be nice if you were in a position to trade off shifts. But you
knocked yourself out with a cocktail of Ambien and vodka.

Group was rough last night. I don't even really want to write
about it, but I need something to do or I'll sit here obsessing about
Jonathan's fever all night. One of our members—Chuck Mandrell,
who lost his only daughter to opioids three months ago—told us his
wife came home from work last Friday and announced she's
leaving him and their twelve-year-old son. She completely blindsided them, says it's simply too painful to be around them anymore.
Chuck's a mess, of course. He feels ashamed he wasn't able to hold
his marriage together in the aftermath of losing his daughter. On
top of that, he's overwhelmed by the legal aspect of getting divorced,
not to mention the daunting task of letting everyone in their circle
know what's happened. He wishes he could lock himself in the
house, so he doesn't have to face anyone.

It was brave of him to come to group, but he knows he can
count on our support. He seems to think his wife's family will

blame him for not being supportive enough of her. Apparently, they blamed him for his daughter's death. They said he worked too much and didn't pay her enough attention, but Chuck told us his wife was always complaining about money and made him take all the overtime he could get. Talk about crazy-making—Chuck's been dealing with it for years.

His story hit home because now he's a single parent raising a son, just like I'll be soon. He says the hardest thing he's facing is convincing his son that he did nothing wrong, that his mother didn't leave because she doesn't love him anymore. That's my fear too, that our son will grow up thinking you left because you didn't love him. Deep down I know you do. You just love the drugs more.

We did our best to console Chuck. Every one of us was hit hard by the curveball life threw our way. It's even more unfair that Chuck's been struck again when he's still reeling from the first blow. I don't know that there's really anything he can tell his son to make him feel better about his mother walking out on him. Only that grief makes people do strange things.

One day our son will be old enough to ask questions. And when that day comes, I don't know if you'll be alive to answer them. It breaks my heart to write those words, but I need to face the harsh truth. We promised to love each other "till death do us part," but it feels as if you're on the fast track to six-feet-under with the choices you're making.

As hard as it is to think of leaving you, it's harder yet to picture what our son will be forced to witness as he grows older if I stay. I can't watch him suffer. I won't let you do to him what you've done to me.

25

PRESENT DAY

I wait until a few days later before executing the next step in my plan. Rick is attending a two-day training seminar with some of his staff, and Lynn mentioned that they were looking for volunteers to clean the community center while they were gone. I tell her I'm happy to help out, smiling inwardly when she gives me a set of keys to open up. A stroke of luck! The timing couldn't be more perfect.

When I arrive, Imelda, a veteran volunteer, is already hard at work scrubbing down the kitchen. She inverts a wiry brow and gives me a curt nod clearly conveying her disapproval. I'm late. I'm not dressed for the job, and I look like I've never done a day's manual work in my life. She would be right on all three counts, but that's irrelevant. I'm here for a job all right, it just doesn't happen to have anything to do with volunteering to clean the community center. It's time to set my plan into motion. As soon as I've managed to plant the evidence in Rick's office, I'll feign an injury and leave Imelda to it. Clearly, she's convinced of her superior cleaning skills and won't appreciate my measly efforts to pitch in.

N. L. HINKENS

"You'll find supplies, and a mop and bucket in that closet right there," she calls to me, pointing with a sudsy yellow glove to the far corner of the kitchen. "I'm almost done wiping down the counters in here, and I plan on tackling the appliances next. You can get started mopping the floor in the main hall and dusting down the stage area." She turns her attention back to the counters which are already gleaming, her brawny arm vibrating with energy as she scrubs back and forth.

Behind Imelda's back, I scowl as I make my way to the closet in question and grab a couple of rags and a bottle of all-purpose cleaning spray. She's an unwelcome distraction, but if I don't satisfy her requirements, she could disrupt my plan. I can't have her hovering over my shoulder the entire time. Holding my breath, I yank out a grimy, wheeled yellow bucket. The mop resting inside it looks like it hasn't been disinfected since the community center first opened its doors. I shudder as I reach for it. I always kept everything so pristine for Jonathan—disinfecting counters, sterilizing bottles, washing all his cloth diapers in eco-friendly detergent. Not that it did any good. None of it kept him alive. I fought to the bitter end in family court for custody, but I lost because a spineless social worker deemed my estranged husband a fit parent. I slam the door shut with such force that Imelda spins around, her over-plucked brows shooting halfway up her forehead.

"Easy," she scolds. "No wonder half the hinges are hanging off around this place."

"Sorry," I mutter, berating myself inwardly. I shouldn't be drawing attention to myself like this. I need Imelda to lose interest in me, and the best way to do that is to get to work as soon as possible. Hopefully, when I sneak off to Rick's office, she won't even notice I'm gone. And, if she does, she'll assume I went to the bathroom. I fill the bucket with industrial floor cleaner and hot water and wheel it out into the main hall. The grubby, scuffed floor seems to stretch forever in every direction. It'll take me at least an hour to mop this place.

I start at the far end and begin working my way across the room toward the corridor where the offices are located. When I hear Imelda take a phone call, I replace the mop in the bucket, grab the bottle of cleaning fluid and a rag, and steal down the hallway to Rick's office. I throw a quick glance in both directions and then twist the doorknob. It's locked, but I have a master key on the ring Lynn gave me. I open the door and slip inside the room, pulling out the card from my pocket. I glance around the room trying to decide on the best place to stash it—somewhere it won't be found until the room is thoroughly searched by the police after Jessica goes missing. I yank out the bottom drawer on the desk and slide the card all the way to the back beneath the hanging files. Unless Rick takes a sudden notion of cleaning out his drawers, the card won't be discovered any time soon. But it won't need to remain hidden for long. Jessica's due date is tomorrow. Shortly after that, she'll disappear. And then things will begin to run amok in the Wests' world.

Satisfied that the card is well-concealed, I slip back out of Rick's office and turn the key in the lock.

"What are you doing?" a male voice calls out.

I pivot to see Jeff, Rick's assistant, coming around the corner. My stomach flips. What on earth is he doing here? I assumed he was at the training seminar with Rick and the rest of the staff.

"Uh, hi, Jeff. I wasn't expecting to see you here. I thought you'd be at the conference."

His frown deepens. I don't like the look he's giving me. He's evaluating me again, like he did when we were first introduced. "Rick and I trade off attending staff training seminars. One of us needs to be on site. Can I help you with something?"

I hold up the bottle of cleaning fluid sheepishly and chuckle. "I volunteered to help clean the center today. I was just going to give the offices a quick wipe down and empty the trash cans."

Jeff folds his arms in front of his chest. "The staff members take care of their own offices. We only ask our volunteers to clean the communal areas."

"Oh, okay. Got it." I give an indifferent shrug. "In that case, I'll check in with Imelda to see what else needs to be done." I turn and walk off down the hallway before he has a chance to question me further. I can feel his eyes burning into my back as I retreat. Jeff doesn't like me. More importantly, he doesn't trust me. And as loyal as he is to Rick, that could be my undoing.

26

SEPTEMBER 28, 2008

oday I visited a divorce attorney to find out what my rights are in regard to custody of Jonathan. I can't expose him to your reckless behavior any longer. It's time to redirect my energy into something I can control—our son's future. I was a basket case the entire time I was in the attorney's office. I liked him though. He was patient and understanding. But he asked me so many questions I didn't anticipate. I thought I would simply have to hand over our bank statements and tax returns and he would file the paperwork and that would pretty much be the end of it. Apparently, it's not that simple. This is going to be a lot more work than I anticipated. He explained the process to me, but I don't think I retained a word he said. I'll have to read through the paperwork he gave me and then call the office with any questions. He mentioned something about trying to work out a temporary arrangement regarding custody until the case is settled. He thinks it would be better for Jonathan if he and I stay in the family home and you move out. I called a couple of people in my therapy group who have young children to ask their opinion about it. They all agreed it would be much better for our son if he and I stay in the family home. So that's what we're going to do. I'm not going to give you too much advance notice. I know you'll go ballistic when I broach the subject.

I really hope you don't contest the divorce and drag this thing out. I don't care about the money—our assets and pensions. I only care about Jonathan. I told the attorney as much, but he said I should do everything in my power to secure our son's financial future, rather than allow you to fritter away funds he might need for college later on. I suppose he's right. If you keep going in the direction you're going in, it's only a matter of time before you lose your job or get arrested.

One thing I do remember from the appointment is that the attorney thinks I have a solid case for sole custody. Based on all the evidence I've been collecting, you'll probably be limited to supervised visits. The attorney recommended hiring a private investigator to follow you on one of your trips downtown to procure drugs. The idea of it doesn't sit well with me, even though I know it's the right thing to do for Jonathan's sake. I can't imagine how I would react if I was denied custody of our son. But maybe this will finally be the push you need to go to rehab. It's not that I want to take Jonathan away from you. Believe me, I'm not enjoying any of this. I hope one day you can come back into his life when you're healthy. I'll always leave that door open.

27

PRESENT DAY

*J*essica is two days past her due date, and it's time she and I had a little conversation. I've lured her over to my place on the pretext of asking her opinion on a new line of clothing I'm thinking of ordering for my store. She's always up for anything that might involve a few fashion freebies.

"Well, what do you think?" I ask, scrolling through some of the wholesale items I've highlighted on my laptop.

"I like the leggings a lot. Not so much the tops. They're meh, nothing exciting."

"Yeah, I kind of feel the same way," I reply. "I think I'll order a few pairs of their leggings and see how they sell first." I close the lid on my laptop and set it aside, studying my nails for a moment. "Jessica, there's something I need to tell you."

She looks up from her phone sharply, taken off guard by my somber tone. "What? You're not backing out on being my labor coach, are you?"

"No, of course not." I blow out a breath as though what I'm about to say has been weighing heavily on me. "I overheard Rick and Lynn bickering the other day—I'm not certain, but I think they were arguing about you."

Jessica pulls nervously at a strand of pink hair. "What were they saying?"

"To be honest, it didn't make much sense to me. Lynn told Rick that he needed to take care of things, to make *her* go away."

A look of alarm crosses Jessica's face. "Did they say anything else?"

I hesitate, pressing my lips together in an expression of regret. "This is really difficult for me ... I don't know—"

Jessica lays a hand on my arm. "*Please*, I need you to tell me what you heard."

I stare morosely at the floor. "Lynn said they weren't going to hand over a penny—it was bad enough that they would have to raise his child. Rick said something back to her, but it was muffled, and I couldn't make it out. Then she yelled at him that he should have thought of that before he ... before he cheated on her." I turn to Jessica, a suitably stricken look on my face. "What did she mean?"

Jessica's eyes narrow. "They're not going to pay up, that's what she means." She gets to her feet and begins pacing. "I knew I shouldn't have trusted them. They promised me ten grand to turn the baby over to them. I said I wanted the check by my due date, but Rick made some excuse about not making it to the bank on time. He's screwed me over—twice now. I should never have hooked up with him again."

"I ... don't understand. What are you talking about?"

"There is no surrogacy!" Jessica wheels around and glares at me. "You don't know the real Rick West. When I was in the youth program, he plied me with drugs and seduced me. I thought he loved me, until he got engaged to Lynn. That's why I moved away—to try and forget him. When I came back, he told me he'd never stopped loving me, and I stupidly started up an affair with him again. He even bought me more weed! He was dealing years ago, although everyone thought it was me. When I got pregnant, he swore he would leave Lynn as soon as the baby was born. All I had to do was play along with the surrogacy story—be the silent partner—until then. I knew he would never really leave her, but I was counting on that money to make a fresh start."

I stare at Jessica, mouth agape. It's just as I suspected, only worse. Rick West is a lying, cheating, druggie—a con man through and through, just like my estranged husband. And Lynn is protecting him. They need to be punished. It's time to teach them both a lesson they won't forget.

I take a deep breath. "I have an idea. I know how you can turn this around, Jessica. Let me help you."

JESSICA'S WATER breaks the next day. I get her frantic call at 11:35 in the morning and immediately begin going over in my mind the steps I will need to take over the next couple of days. "Calm down, Jess," I soothe. "Everything's going to be fine. Remember what we talked about." I suck on my bottom lip for a moment and then add, "You have the information, right?"

"Yes, it's in my purse."

"Okay, I'll grab my stuff and be right over."

"Hurry, please," Jessica says sounding panic-stricken. "I'm having regular contractions."

I hang up and reach for the duffel bag that's been packed and waiting by my front door for weeks. After adding my laptop and charging cord, I drape my purse over my shoulder and head out to my car. I throw my stuff on the back seat and then jog next door.

Jessica is pacing back and forth over the kitchen floor. "I've made a huge mess. I threw a couple of towels down."

"Forget it. It's not important. Where's your bag?"

She gestures at the door where her jacket is folded atop a small rolling carry-on case.

After I've loaded her things into the car, I help her out of the house and down the driveway. She makes her way gingerly to the curb and waits for me to open the passenger door.

I reach for her by the elbow and guide her in. "You can do this, Jess."

Groaning, she slides onto the seat, contorting in pain.

"Just breathe through it," I say quietly, resting a hand on her shoulder.

Once the contraction has passed, I waste no time jumping behind the wheel and peeling away from the curb. I shoot Jessica a quick sideways glance. "Doing better?"

She nods, eyes closed, and leans back against the seat. "It's over, for now. Hurry, please."

We drive in silence for a moment or two and then Jessica reaches into her purse and pulls out a slip of paper. "This is my account number and the address I'll be at."

Wordlessly, I take the note from her and slip it into my pocket.

She turns and stares at me. "Will you call him Jonathan?"

OCTOBER 03, 2008

*B*eing vulnerable leads to being hurt. And I'm already in enough pain. So that's why I chose to isolate myself more and more instead of reaching out to friends early on. I've closed the door on casual inquiries into your whereabouts or well-being. Why? Because I was too ashamed to tell them the truth about your drug use. I was afraid they would judge us. And I didn't want to bother them with your self-inflicted problems. Instead, I worked hard to maintain the facade of a happy marriage and tried to minimize the consequences of your behavior. I told friends you were stressed out and exhausted beyond belief because of your demanding job. It sounded so much more acceptable than the dark and twisted truth. I didn't want them all gossiping about us behind our backs. It's like we failed somehow. There's a certain stigma about middle-class people and substance abuse. If you don't come from the gutter, you shouldn't have those types of problems. Only people who sleep on benches and drink out of paper bags are addicts. I kept hoping against hope that this would end soon, that you would come to your senses. But your addiction is only picking up speed and aggression as the weeks go by. It's beyond frustrating to watch you retreat to your toxic fortress night after night.

They all know now, of course, what's going on with you, but by the time I came clean with everyone around me, it was too late to salvage relationships I'd neglected for so long. It's been a hard lesson for me. It's one thing for you to lose your friends—you chose drugs over them, so you have no one to blame but yourself. But I've suffered relationship losses too because of your choices. You forced me to become as secretive in my daily life as you. We were both living a double life, little white lies that grew a tangled hedge of protection between us and the world around us. I lost the trust of my friends. I wish now that I'd invited them in and let them help me at the very beginning. I get a lump in my throat when I think of how much covering for you has cost me. I've lost several close friends over the last few months. Too much baggage and too much drama make a scary equation. They said all the right things after I confided in them initially, offered to meet up for coffee, brought over casseroles, promised to support me in whatever way they could. But in the end, they either gradually put distance between us, or dumped me outright. I guess they got tired of me not returning their calls or bailing out last minute on our plans. Their idea of helping was to go out and have fun, to try and cheer me up. They had good intentions. I don't harbor any resentment toward them. They didn't know that it wasn't safe to leave you alone with Jonathan.

29

PRESENT DAY

hree days later, I wake up to a loud banging on my front door, interspersed by someone repeatedly ringing the doorbell. For a moment I lie there motionless trying to remember what day it is, and then it hits me like the roar of a crashing wave. Jessica came home from the hospital yesterday with a healthy baby boy, seven-pounds-eleven-ounces, twenty-one inches long.

I rub my eyes and sit bolt upright in bed. Glancing at my phone on the dresser I see that it's 6:35 a.m. If everything has gone according to plan, Jessica is officially missing. I stumble out of bed and tie my robe around my waist, taking a moment to arrange my expression into one of sleepy confusion. I'm guessing either Rick or Lynn is hammering on my front door looking for her. Naturally, they would come here first. After all, I was Jessica's birth partner and we've been spending a lot of time together lately.

I make a half-hearted attempt to smooth down my hair as I hurry down the stairs and pull open the front door. A frantic Lynn stares back at me, bug-eyed and trembling. Before I can say a word, she thrusts a sheet of paper at me.

"Jessica's gone, and she's taken our baby. She left this on the counter."

I stagger backward and let my jaw drop. I've practiced my reaction to this news a thousand times over in my mind—the stunned neighbor, woken out of a deep sleep in the early hours, uncomprehending at first, then reeling from shock, offering sympathy, assistance, comfort, perhaps even a drink of water to my enemy. The irony of it isn't lost on me. My lawyer offered me a paper cup of water after he informed me I had lost custody of Jonathan. I stare down at the note, blinking as I pretend to read it through. But I know the words by heart. I penned them for Jessica who painstakingly copied them out in her own handwriting—an overly emotional outpouring explaining how she's changed her mind and wants to keep her baby after all, begging the Wests not to look for her, telling them they can keep their money.

Lynn pulls nervously at her ear. "I'm so worried about the baby. I know Jessica's been smoking weed again. Did she mention anything to you about leaving?" Lynn's voice is plaintive, hungry for a morsel of information, some indication that I might know something that could help her. I understand the level of desperation she's feeling as her baby slowly slips from her grasp. This is so much better than anything else I could have done to her—it's a living death of sorts.

Shaking my head, I meet her stricken gaze. If the eyes are truly the gateway to the soul, then she ought to be able to read the truth in mine—that there's no empathy there. I'm not mourning her loss. I'm celebrating my victory. But her own eyes are too blurred with tears to see what's right in front of her.

"I'm so sorry, Lynn," I say breathlessly. "I can't believe Jessica would pull something like this after everything you've done for her." I hand her back the note. "What are you going to do? Have you called the police yet?"

Lynn's eyes widen. "The police? No, there's no point. They can't force her to come back. I mean, we didn't have an official contract for the surrogacy or anything. It was just a verbal agreement."

I play along and arch a surprised brow. "Surely you must have had something in writing. Didn't Jessica insist you commit to covering her medical costs before she agreed to act as your surrogate?"

Lynn claws at her cheek, looking increasingly flustered. "It's complicated. Rick knew her from the youth program, so we thought we could trust her."

I rub my forehead, pretending to think this through. "Do you think she might have gone to a family member, or maybe to her ex-boyfriend's place?"

Lynn shakes her head. "No, she doesn't have any family. Her father's in prison, and she hasn't been in touch with her mother for years. And she wouldn't go back to her ex-boyfriend's."

No, she wouldn't. Because there is no ex-boyfriend, as Jessica confided to me a few days ago. The whole story about being kicked out in the middle of the night was simply a tale Lynn and Rick concocted to explain why she was moving in with them. I furrow my brow, reveling in my advisory role. "I still think you should call the police. I mean, Jessica just gave birth, she's not thinking straight. And if she's using again … she … *they* could be in danger. I mean, I hate to be so blunt about it, but a dopehead can't be trusted to care for a newborn."

Lynn's face pales. "You're right. I'll talk to Rick about calling the police."

I give an approving nod. "Keep me posted. I'll let you

know if I hear anything from Jessica. Have you tried calling her cell phone?"

"It's been disconnected," Lynn replies, her voice wobbling.

Another fact I'm well aware of. It's been disconnected because Jessica has a new phone, and a new number, just like she has a new life now. "That's odd," I say. "I don't like the sound of that. You don't think she'd deliberately harm herself, do you? Or the baby?"

Lynn's hand flies to her lips. "Don't say that!"

"I'm sorry, I'm not trying to alarm you any further. It's just that something's obviously wrong. She could be suffering from postpartum depression. And with her history of drug abuse … " I chew on my lip for a moment, letting the ominous message sink in. "I think you should call 911 right away."

With a fleeting nod, Lynn darts back across the lawn and disappears inside her house.

I flop down in a chair in the family room, my arms dangling over the armrests. I feel euphoric, endorphins flowing freely like I'm high on something myself. My performance was flawless, utterly convincing. Soon the police will be here, interviewing the neighbors, searching for a missing person. Annie and Charles will share their suspicions about the Wests. I will turn over my edited recording. The diary will be found on Jessica's laptop detailing the affair and the drugs. Rick's home and office will be searched. Once the police find the card in his file drawer and verify Jessica's signature, they will suspect foul play. It will only be a matter of time before Lynn is a blubbering mess. I look forward to watching her world fall apart around her.

30

OCTOBER 25, 2008

I finally broke down and drove two hours to my parents' place yesterday to tell them the truth about your addiction. I spared them the explicit details, but I didn't minimize the extent of the problem. They were speechless at first, confused, not believing what they were hearing. That's what happens when someone is blindsided by news like this. You always came across as the perfect spouse, the consummate professional who had everything together. After I answered all their questions, and explained that I was going to leave you, they got angry. Mom yelled at me, completely distraught, and then she burst into tears. "I don't understand," she sobbed over and over again. "How did this happen? How could you have let this happen under your own roof? My grandson deserves better than a broken home."

I felt so helpless as I watched the tears rolling down Mom's face. I relate to her distress only too well. I've wrestled with those same tangled emotions for the past few months—that three-pronged pitchfork of frustration, confusion, and rage. And the never-ending questions. What could I have done differently? Why didn't I realize it sooner? How is all of this going to affect Jonathan? I don't have any good answers.

I wish I knew what drove you to addiction. Were you discontent? Were you missing something in our relationship? You've never offered me a good explanation. I thought all along we were happy together, you, me and Jonathan. As far as I was concerned, we had it all.

Dad was more stoic in his response. Twenty years in the military taught him a level of self-control Mom has never been able to master. He asked all the practical questions. Had you ever been arrested? Are you dipping into our savings to fund your habit? Did you ever put Jonathan in harm's way? I hesitated a moment too long before answering that last one. He knew I was hedging, reluctant to throw you under the bus. His drawn expression masked the storm of emotions inside, fists clenching and unclenching at his sides, searching for a way to make things better like he always does. But he can't make this better. Only you can do that.

After Mom had calmed down a bit, we discussed the situation. Bouncing a few ideas off my parents helped clarify things for me moving forward. I feel like I have a solid game plan now. Before I left to drive back home, they assured me of their support and even offered Jonathan and me a place to stay if we needed it. They want to help in whatever way they can. They're disappointed in you and hurt for me, of course. But more than anything they're scared for Jonathan. And they should be.

31

PRESENT DAY

I make myself an espresso and savor it as I collect my thoughts while keeping an eye out the window on any developments next door. No doubt Lynn and Rick are arguing about whether or not to call the police. Rick has a lot to hide. Once it comes to light that he supplied Jessica with weed, he'll be out of a job and facing charges. The last thing he needs is cops crawling all over his house sifting through potential evidence that might implicate him in Jessica's disappearance. But Lynn, ever the rescuer, and worried about the baby, will advocate for alerting law enforcement and, despite all of Rick's objections, is unlikely to take no for an answer.

It's still too early to call Annie, but I'm looking forward to breaking the news to her that Jessica has disappeared, and then waiting for her to connect the dots. I need to make sure she thinks it's her idea that Rick and Lynn might have done something to harm Jessica. And then I'll supply my supporting evidence to encourage Annie to share her suspicions with the police. It won't matter if she wants to talk it over with Charles first. He'll convince her to notify the

103

authorities. After that, I can rely on Annie, my unwitting accomplice, to inform the entire neighborhood of the burgeoning scandal. It won't be long before Rick and Lynn West will be unable to leave their house without being accosted by irate neighbors demanding justice for Jessica, and local news reporters jostling for an exclusive.

Twenty minutes go by, and a squad car pulls up next door. A young, thick-necked officer in mirrored sunglasses climbs out and strolls nonchalantly up to the front door. His body language oozes apathy. He's not taking this seriously yet, and why would he? Jessica's not a minor, and, strictly speaking, she's not a runaway either. She's not even related to Rick and Lynn, and they may not have told the police about their phony surrogacy arrangement, in which case the baby hasn't technically been abducted. I wish I could be a fly on the wall and listen in on how they explain the situation to the officer.

I drain my cup, my thoughts turning once again to Jonathan. The sweet smell of his newborn skin lingers in my nostrils even after all this time. I couldn't save my son, but I can still save Jessica's baby. And maybe in the process, Jessica's baby will save me.

I'm unloading the dishwasher when my doorbell rings for the second time this morning. I take a moment to compose myself before opening the door. The young officer I saw pull up to the curb earlier is standing on my doorstep. He removes his mirrored sunglasses and scrutinizes me. "Are you Nora Munroe?"

I nod mutely, painting a perplexed expression on my face. Inside, my heart is thudding furiously, the way it always does when I'm around cops.

"I'm Officer Dufour," he says. "Your next-door neighbors, Rick and Lynn West, reported their tenant missing a little while ago. I understand you were friendly with her. Can I take a few minutes of your time to ask you some questions?"

"Uh, yes, of course." I usher him inside and lead him through to the family room.

He eyes the moving boxes curiously as he takes a seat and pulls out a small notebook. "Can you tell me when you last saw Jessica?"

I sit down opposite him and stare at the carpet, frowning. "Yesterday, around two-thirty or three in the afternoon. I went over there to check on her and see the baby."

"Mr. and Mrs. West mentioned that Jessica had grown quite attached to you over the past few months. I understand she even spent the night here on several occasions."

I give a small shrug of acknowledgement.

Officer Dufour regards me intently, waiting on me to elaborate on the statement he's left hanging, but I won't let myself be drawn into giving away too much. I've watched enough police shows to know that people incriminate themselves when they talk too much. I'll stick to answering his questions as succinctly as possible while taking every opportunity to lead him in the direction I want him to go.

He bounces his knee up and down for a moment or two as if considering how to proceed, or maybe he's just bored with the uneventful incident he's been called out to investigate. Little does he know things are about to get a whole lot more interesting.

Officer Dufour taps a finger on his chin. "Did Jessica ever mention having second thoughts about becoming a surrogate?"

I press down on my lips. So, Rick and Lynn spun the surrogacy story after all. I tilt my head to one side, attempting to look pensive. "Not directly, but ... I think she felt obligated."

"Obligated? Do you mean pressured?" Officer Dufour's

tone has become sharper, his gaze predatory. He's young, driven, hungry to unearth a potential crime in a sleepy neighborhood. He's perfect for what I have in mind.

"Now that you mention it, one of our other neighbors did say Jessica complained a lot about how controlling the Wests were. They made her work in the community center where Rick works in return for room and board."

Officer Dufour frowns and scribbles something down in his notebook. "What's this neighbor's name?"

"Annie Edmonds. She lives a few doors down from me. She's kind of like everyone's grandma around here, so people tend to confide in her."

Officer Dufour gives a contemptuous grunt. "Is there anything else at all you can think of that might be helpful?"

"Well—" I wave my hand dismissively. "It's probably nothing."

He leans forward. "Sometimes even the smallest things can prove useful in these kinds of cases."

I force a stiff smile. Exactly how many of "these kinds of cases" has he cracked? He looks like he's only been on the job for a year or two at most. "It's nothing more than a hunch really," I say with a sheepish shrug. "It's just that something about the surrogacy never seemed right to me. I'm not sure Rick and Lynn are being completely honest about everything."

The doorbell rings before Officer Dufour can respond.

"I'd better get that," I say, trying to curb my irritation at being interrupted before I could drop my bombshell. "It might be Lynn again."

He nods. "Go ahead, I'll wait."

When I pull open the door, I'm surprised to see Annie standing on my doorstep. I haven't had a chance to call her yet, but this could work in my favor. I might not even need to play my doctored recording for Officer Dufour if Annie is convincing enough.

"Oh Nora, isn't it awful?" she exclaims, one hand fluttering around her face like a butterfly seeking a place to alight. "Lynn called me in a terrible state asking if I'd seen Jessica."

I reach for her arm. "Come in out of the cold. There's an officer here asking questions about Jessica's disappearance."

Annie peers past me, a gleam of curiosity in her eyes. She lowers her voice to what she deems a whisper but is easily loud enough for Officer Dufour's ears to pick up. "Maybe I should come back later."

"No, he'll want to talk to you too. He's interviewing all the neighbors."

Annie presses her lips together and allows me to escort her to the family room where I introduce her to Officer Dufour. "This is Annie Edmonds, the neighbor I was telling you about."

He gives a curt nod of acknowledgement. "I hope you don't mind if I ask you a few questions while you're here."

Annie takes a seat and smooths down her skirt. "Not at all. Naturally, I'm only too willing to help. It's shocking to think a young woman could just disappear like that."

"Indeed." Officer Dufour consults his notebook. "Mrs. Edmonds, did Jessica seem happy living with the Wests, in your opinion?"

Annie purses her lips and shoots me a quick glance. "Well, to be perfectly frank, I think she found them a bit controlling. They were always telling her when to be home, and where she could go, and what she should eat, and all that kind of stuff. Young people don't like to be told what to do at the best of times, and I'm sure with all those hormones raging ... well, let's just say it made for some battles between them. And then, of course, they made the poor girl work in the kitchen over at the community center. It's a wonder her ankles didn't swell up. When I was pregnant with—"

"If I may stop you there, Mrs. Edmonds, did Jessica ever indicate to you that she had changed her mind about giving the Wests her baby?"

The folds in Annie's brow deepen. "No, I can't say she did, but then she'd hardly have mentioned that to me. She knew I was friendly with Rick and Lynn. I used to volunteer at the community center when I was younger, you see, until it all got to be too much for me."

Officer Dufour notes something down on his pad. "And when did you last see Jessica?"

"Yesterday, mid-morning I believe. I took her over some of my chicken noodle soup. Of course, I really wanted a peek at the baby. He is a gorgeous little thing, the biggest blue eyes you've ever seen and—"

"Yes, the Wests gave me a description." Officer Dufour flips his notebook closed. "Thank you for your time, Mrs. Edmonds. Here's my card in case you think of anything else." He nods in my direction. "I'll see myself out."

A moment later the front door creaks open and then closes. Annie pockets the officer's card, shaking her head sadly. "Just think, Nora, you predicted this. You said Jessica might disappear one day."

3 2

NOVEMBER 05, 2008

*A*ddiction and divorce go hand-in-hand. I read that on the internet so it must be true, right? Supposedly I'm not to blame myself for the dissolution of our marriage because addicts are self-destructive. They destroy all their relationships and then blame everyone around them for the fallout. It's a pattern I recognize. You lie to me constantly and then attack me for doubting you. But what do you expect? You forced me to stop trusting you a long time ago. I have to protect our son, and right now he's not safe around you.

Speaking of trust, I haven't told you yet that I'm planning to divorce you. I feel somewhat guilty about keeping it from you, but I'm following my attorney's advice to wait until I've collected the evidence I need. If I give you a heads up, you might start covering your tracks. The private investigator the attorney hired has been following you around for several weeks now. You have no clue you're being tailed. You're so completely consumed with your habit, most of the time you're oblivious to everyone around you. He has video of you illegally purchasing drugs on the street. You'd be shocked if you knew that. I feel kind of weird about the idea of hiring someone to surveil you, but you've left me no choice. I can't *risk you getting joint custody of Jonathan. Not that there's much chance of that happening. A few days ago, the PI managed to intercept your email and found evidence of several illegal electronic transactions of drug purchases. Together with the photographs I've got of your fraudulent prescriptions, and of you passed out on the couch next to your pills, it should be easy enough to sway the court in my favor.*

At our last appointment, my attorney brought up the topic of a restraining order. I admit I was taken aback. I told him it was completely unnecessary. You've never raised a hand to me. Sure, you've gotten angry in the past and yelled when I confronted you, but you've never become physical. Regardless, the attorney was adamant that I need to be prepared to take action in case everything changes once I serve you with divorce papers. I'm dreading taking that final step.

I just found out that a social worker was assigned to our case this week. Supposedly, she'll be making an unannounced visit to the house at some point. If she comes when you're out, I'm going to show her all the places where you hide your prescription bottles—I found the stash taped beneath your office drawer, by the way. Clever, but not very original. If you're here when she shows up, I'll have no choice but to tell you I'm leaving. It's time you knew anyway.

My divorce attorney has worked with this particular social worker before—he seems to think she's competent. So long as she does her job, it will suffice. I don't need her sympathy, just her support to win custody of Jonathan.

33

PRESENT DAY

*a*nnie has turned out to be an excellent asset. The suspicions she relayed to Officer Dufour have served to ratchet up the investigation to the next level. I watch from behind a curtain as Rick and Lynn pull out of their driveway and follow Officer Dufour's squad car down the street. No doubt they've been asked to go down to the station to give a statement. They might even have retained a lawyer. Anticipation tingles inside me. Things will move quickly now. It's time to implement the next step of my plan, and for that I need Daisy's help.

I remove a meaty bone I bought at the butcher's from my refrigerator and stuff a plastic bag into my pocket. Equipped with a trowel I purchased a few days ago at the hardware store, I scurry outside and let myself into the Wests' back yard through their side gate. I work quickly, burying the bone behind a weeping willow tree in a hole that's deep enough to prevent Daisy from digging it up too easily. By the time DNA rules out human remains, the Wests' lives will be in tatters. And I've only just begun.

I pick up Daisy from Charles' house at my usual time. We

spend several minutes talking in hushed tones about Jessica's disappearance. I shed a few crocodile tears and Charles gives me an awkward hug, trying to reassure me that the police will find her. After drying my eyes, I put Daisy on the leash and take her to the park. Instead of hanging out and playing with her for any length of time as we usually do, I walk her straight back to my street. I ring Rick's and Lynn's doorbell to make sure they haven't returned, and then make my way around the side of the house into their backyard. With a gentle tug of the leash, I lead Daisy over to the far end of the lawn behind the weeping willow tree. Immediately, her nose is to the ground, sniffing excitedly, her tail taut as she evaluates the intoxicating smell wafting her way. Her little paws begin to dig frantically at the loose dirt, but to her immense dismay, I pick her up and interrupt her saliva-inducing excavation project.

"Let's go home and tell Daddy what we found, shall we?" I say, kissing the top of her little head. Her reaction is everything I hoped for and more. Ignoring her yelps of protest, I carry her back out to the street and set her down. Resigned to the course I have set, Daisy trots along obediently at my heel. Once we turn the corner onto Ash Street, I switch off my phone in preparation for the little scenario I have planned. Charles rarely remembers to charge his cell phone, so he won't find it odd if I tell him my battery's dead when he asks to use my phone to alert the police to the fact that something suspicious is buried in the Wests' backyard.

I find him parked in his mushroom-colored leather swivel chair, his wire-rimmed reading glasses perched at the tip of his nose as he peruses the newspaper. He looks up in surprise when I open the slider door.

"Did you wear her out already?" he asks, patting his leg in an invitation to Daisy to join him.

I let her off the leash but don't respond to his question.

Charles makes the requisite fuss over Daisy, and then peers at me questioningly. "Are you all right, Nora? You're very quiet."

I sink down in the wing-backed chair opposite him. "To tell you the truth, I'm not sure."

He removes his glasses and places them on the end table next to his chair. "I know you're upset about Jessica leaving with the baby and—"

I cut him off with a wave of my hand. "It's not that."

Charles rubs Daisy's ear and blinks solemnly at me. "What's wrong then?"

I bite my lip and hold his penetrating gaze for a moment or two before answering. "I'm still trying to figure that out. I went next door on my way back from the park to see if by any chance Jessica had returned. I rang the front doorbell and then went around the back to check if she was in her flat. When I got to the bottom of the garden, Daisy started going crazy, digging and sniffing at some loose dirt behind a tree. I … I don't know … I mean, it made me very uncomfortable. You know, in light of everything—Jessica disappearing in the middle of the night and all."

Charles' eyes narrow. He presses his lips together tightly as he pushes himself up from his armchair. "Show me this spot you're talking about."

"You don't think—" I halt mid-sentence and press my fist to my lips.

He grimaces. "I don't think anything, yet. I need to see what you're talking about for myself."

He exchanges his slippers for a pair of tennis shoes and dons his wide-brimmed hat. Cane in hand, he clips Daisy's leash back on and locks up the house behind us.

For her part, Daisy appears quite content to be heading out for a second time in the space of a few short hours. Her ears are pert, her little head swiveling like a baby bird at every sight and sound that catches her attention. When we reach the Wests' house, I make a show of ringing the doorbell again even though their car's not back yet. "No one home," I say to Charles with a small shrug.

He nods and walks around to the back yard. I follow a few steps behind as he shuffles his way down to the bottom of the garden. He hasn't even reached the willow tree when Daisy begins straining on the leash. Right on cue, she heads straight for the same spot and sniffs excitedly, doing her best to dig up the loose dirt as Charles tugs her back.

"Do you want me to fetch a spade or something?" I ask in a breathless whisper.

"No!" Charles' tone is sharp and abrupt. He pulls his bushy brows into a stiff frown. "We can't touch anything. It's important we don't destroy any evidence."

I suck in an audible breath, another dramatic skill I've practiced ad nauseam in front of the mirror. "You don't really believe … " I stare, mouth agape, at the spot where Daisy was digging, leaving the insinuation to speak for itself.

Charles balls his free hand into a gnarled fist. "Wouldn't take much dirt to bury an infant."

I clap a hand over my mouth as if I'm about to retch. In reality, my fingers are masking the smile breaking out across my face. The bone is the perfect red herring to elevate the cloud of suspicion surrounding Rick. With a bit of luck, the police will conjecture that Jessica's baby was buried here, and that Rick moved the body. It's not looking good for him, no matter what angle the police take.

"I hope I'm wrong about this, but my gut's telling me I should call it in, " Charles says, his face set in a grim scowl. "Do you have your phone on you?"

I scrabble around in my pocket and pull it out, staring at the screen in dismay. "My battery's dead."

"Don't worry about it. You go on home, Nora. You're upset enough. I'll take care of this."

We walk around the side of the Wests' house together and Charles pats me on the arm before trundling off down the road. As soon as he disappears around the corner, I scan the street for any signs of life. I can't risk being seen going back into the Wests' yard before the police get here. When I'm satisfied the coast is clear, and that no one is peering through a window at me, I slip around the side of the house once again. After retrieving the trowel from where I stashed it behind a trash can earlier, I hurriedly dig up the bone and toss it into the plastic bag I had stuffed in my pocket. Then, I flatten out the dirt with my hands before throwing the bag over the fence into my garden and retracing my steps.

Once I retrieve the bag, I drop it into my outdoor garbage can, covering it as best I can with an overstuffed bag of smelly trash from the kitchen. It should be enough to mask the odor from Daisy's perceptive little nose if she happens to find her way out here for any reason. My little canine accomplice was marvelous in her starring role. Now it's up to her master to finish what she started and convince the police that something suspicious is buried in the Wests' back yard.

34

I pulled out my journal yesterday, planning to write, but then I realized it was the thirteenth. As stupid as it sounds, I thought it might be unlucky to journal about this nightmare on the thirteenth. The wistful part of me is still hoping for a miracle. But I've been in denial for far too long about how bad the situation is. Or maybe I'm just too scared to put a label on what's really happening, and what's going to happen—our impending divorce. I dread the fallout, picking up the pieces, the sheer enormity of coming to terms with all the repercussions. But the truth is, it can't be any worse than living like this. You're starting to fall apart at the seams. You've lost two credit cards recently. You missed your first day of work last week. And yesterday you fell asleep sitting on the toilet seat when you were supposed to be getting ready to go out to see a movie with me and Jonathan. I was so disgusted, I left you there. I was still fuming at the start of the matinee, but then I realized that this is my life now. I need to embrace every moment with our son instead of depriving him of my attention because I'm too fixated on you and the things I have no control over.

I'm still a coward at heart when it comes to tackling hard things face on. But at least I can honestly say I never stopped trying to make things better as long as we were still together. It's been exhausting trying to save you from yourself. Even my own parents judge me for staying with you for this long. It was one thing when I didn't know about the drugs. But they're horrified that I knowingly continue to put their grandson in danger.

It's easy to judge, it's much harder to decide what consequences are justifiable. That's why I've struggled so long with the idea of leaving you. It feels like I'm abandoning you to this disease. If it is a disease at all. That's a matter of hot debate among the so-called experts. I go back and forth between the two positions myself. We don't choose to inflict a disease on ourselves, but you are choosing to abuse drugs. You've allowed yourself to become dependent on them. How is that not a choice? On the other hand, I don't see this as some kind of character flaw in you. I know you love our son. I know you wouldn't deliberately choose drugs over him. You wouldn't choose to put him in harm's way. It's as if the part of your brain that makes good choices is broken. Getting high has taken on a life of its own and you can't break free.

35

PRESENT DAY

A short while later, the cops arrive with cadaver dogs in tow. My lips curve into a contented smile as I watch them descend on my neighbors' back yard. Charles's concerns were taken seriously—hardly surprising given his long career in law enforcement. But the cadaver dogs will be sorely disappointed by the wild goose chase I've staged for them. I observe the proceedings with interest from the upstairs window of a back bedroom of my house. While the dogs are following their noses around the garden, Officer Dufour opens up the door to Jessica's flat. It will only be a matter of time before he goes through Jessica's few possessions and discovers her laptop. I returned it after I finished editing her diary recounting a lurid affair with Rick—using details she gave me herself; places, dates, even the terms of endearment he favored. Rick won't be able to deny the affair in the face of such compelling evidence, and neither will Lynn anymore. All the world will know that she failed to reform her man. She never could bring herself to label a loser when she saw one. I warned my lawyer time and time again that my husband was a druggie who would endanger our son's life, but Lynn vouched for him, ignoring all my written statements to the court.

I startle out of my reverie when Officer Dufour exits Jessica's flat carrying her laptop in a plastic evidence bag. He strides around the side of the house, all the while talking into his radio. My heart drums faster. It won't be long before the cops find the diary. They have all the evidence they need now to arrest Rick. Or at least to get a warrant to search his house and place of work. My heartbeat quickens when I picture them pulling out the card I hid in his desk drawer. It's such a hopelessly romantic notion that Rick would risk hanging onto a physical card from Jessica. Everyone knows if you want to get away with a crime, you should keep your emotions in check. They always come back to haunt you.

Annie rings my doorbell again shortly after all the ruckus has died down and the police have departed with their dogs. As soon as I open the door to her, I can tell she has news she's dying to relay to me. "I'm parched," she announces without preamble. "Be a dear and put the kettle on."

I usher her into the kitchen and make her a cup of weak tea—the way she likes it. Whatever morsel of information she has gleaned won't be news to me. I have orchestrated this production and I know exactly what comes next.

"I just talked to Imelda Lopez," Annie begins, nursing her mug in her lap. "She was cleaning the community center this morning when the police arrived. Apparently, they cordoned off the entire building and searched every room." Annie pauses, savoring the air of mystery she assumes she has evoked. "Imelda bumped into them coming out of Rick's office carrying a plastic evidence bag with a red card inside. She said there was a sexy image of a girl wearing stilettos and little else on the front of the card—*very* provocative." Annie sips her tea with a satisfied look on her face. "It can't have been from Lynn or the police wouldn't have taken it as evidence. I bet he's been carrying on with Jessica this whole time. Like I always said, Rick's too smooth for his own good." She shakes her head and makes a tutting sound. "It's Lynn I feel sorry for. This will kill her. And after everything she did for him, getting him on the straight and narrow."

"Maybe she knew all along," I say casually stirring my tea.

Annie gives a disapproving grunt. "I find that hard to believe. Lynn's a strait-laced sort. Those social workers always are. She wouldn't have stood for it."

I press my cup to my lips to prevent myself from retorting. I'm tempted to tell Annie what I really think of social workers, especially the kind who live in a fantasy world and insist on believing the best of everyone. People like Lynn are as dangerous as the killers they let go free.

LYNN ARRIVES BACK at the house just as it's getting dark. I hear her car pull up outside and then her garage door rolls open. Rick isn't with her. I drum my fingers on the kitchen counter trying to decide if I should go over there or wait and see if she rings my doorbell first. It's important for me to keep abreast of the investigation while coming across as the concerned neighbor. I need to find out whether or not Rick has been arrested in connection with Jessica's disappearance. At the very least, he is still being held for questioning, which is a good sign. I wait another five minutes or so and then, unable to contain myself any longer, make my way next door and ring the doorbell. I shuffle impatiently from one foot to the other until Lynn peeks cautiously around the curtain in the family room to see who's outside. No doubt she's afraid the press have got wind of Jessica's disappearance. I give her a reassuring wave, and a moment later, the door opens.

Lynn's close-set eyes are sunken and red-rimmed, and her hair hangs listlessly around her pale face. She was never attractive at the best of times, but now she looks decidedly sickly and defeated. I feel proud that I have engineered her demise. Nothing will bring Jonathan back, but maybe the gnawing emptiness inside me will slowly start to subside as justice is served.

"Oh, Lynn, I'm so sorry," I say, as she motions me inside.

She blinks, fighting to keep her tears at bay. "Thanks," she rasps. "I don't think any of it's hit me yet. I'm still in shock." She leads me into the family room and sinks down on her tufted couch, absentmindedly clutching a fringed throw pillow to her chest.

I stare at it, filled with a profound sense of satisfaction that she'll never hold Rick's child next to her beating heart.

"Where's Rick?" I ask, snapping myself out of my self-indulgent thoughts.

"They're still holding him. They released me, but ... " Her voice begins to wobble and then trails off.

"But what?" I nudge, eager to hear her spell out her own misery.

She shakes her head, tears sliding freely down her cheeks. "He was having an affair with Jessica."

"What?" My gasp is so convincing, I almost persuade myself I'm hearing the news for the first time.

"I thought it was only a one-night stand. At least that's what he told me when Jessica called him to let him know she was pregnant. Rick and I agreed to stay together and raise the child. It was my idea to tell everyone that Jessica was our surrogate—she was happy to accept a payout in return. I wanted to protect my husband from ... from any fallout in the community."

I assume a distraught expression. In reality, I'm irate that once again she is choosing to defend a scumbag who doesn't deserve protection, let alone a child. "I don't know what to say."

Lynn wipes the back of her hand across her eyes, choking out a sob. "The police think Rick did something to Jessica. They found a diary on her laptop detailing the affair. And they also found a card in his office that she gave him." Lynn buries her face in her hands. "I just don't understand why they think he had anything to do with her disappearance. He wouldn't lie about something like that."

I look away, hiding my expression of disgust. Is Lynn West really that gullible? Druggies are above average liars. They lie for a living—it's instinctual. I know all about it. I fight to keep my composure as I turn back to face her. "I wish there was something I could do to help. This must be so heartbreaking for you—losing the baby, and now Rick."

She jerks her head up and stares blankly at me through her tears. "I'm not going to lose Rick. He didn't do anything to Jessica. Having an affair is not a criminal offense."

I let my shoulders drop in an apologetic shrug. "He lied about the affair, Lynn. What if that's not all he lied about?"

A nerve twitches in her temple. I can see the fight draining out of her rapidly blinking eyes. She knows I'm right.

I have brought my enemy to her knees.

36

NOVEMBER 18, 2008

elieve me when I say I tried everything to help you before I threw in the towel. I need you to know that. And I want Jonathan to know that one day too—that I didn't give up on you easily. I could have written you off as soon as I found out you were abusing prescription drugs. Instead of showering you with condemnation, I tried to treat you with compassion. I read up on how best to approach a family member addicted to drugs, what to say and what not to say. I tried not to make empty threats. I worked hard to persuade you to change your ways, then encouraged you to get professional help. I even researched what it would be like to come off drugs so I'd be prepared for the withdrawal symptoms you would go through—the chills, the shakes, the nausea. I wanted to be there for you through it all. I sent you hundreds of texts and emails with links to articles you never read. I had countless conversations with you, pleading, scolding, sobbing—at times trying to guilt you into recovery, I admit. I've had countless more conversations with you in my head going over all the ways and times you've hurt me, but I tried not to lash out at you. I combed through addiction forums and studied all the recovery stories always hoping to find some new nugget that would make it all better. But there is no miracle pill, no magic wand to fix this.

All this enabling I've been doing isn't good for either of us. I'm supposed to let you hit rock bottom, so you'll be more motivated to seek treatment. As far as I'm concerned, you're already there. If only you could see how pale and sleep-deprived you've become. You've even lost interest in going to the gym. But it's not enough that I can see the end coming. I have to wait until you're sick and tired of being sick and tired. I've no idea how long that's going to take. I'm terrified you're going to end up homeless once the judge orders you to leave. That's the latest thing I've been Googling— homelessness. I can't stay off the internet, despite my best intentions. Do you have any idea how incredibly dangerous sleeping rough on the streets is? You could die of hypothermia or heatstroke. And there are all sorts of health risks. Not to mention the violence and crime that goes on. I know I'm obsessing again over something that's completely out of my control. It's all morose speculation anyway. It might never come to that.

It's tough for both of us to break the cycles we've been in for so long. Trying to power through has depleted me mentally and physically. I thought I was strong, and in many ways I am, but I can't do this anymore. Nothing I've said or done has made you stop using or lying to me. The only way this is going to change is because you want to change. It's that simple. And equal parts frustrating.

37

PRESENT DAY

*R*ick is out on bail. It was to be expected. After all, there are no bodies, so the police have no direct evidence of foul play—only Jessica's diary, the card, and the note she left behind indicating that she's changed her mind and decided to keep the baby. As far as the police are concerned, she's an adult and free to move wherever she wants to, whenever she wants. But Rick's career is over. With all the rumors flying back and forth about his drug-dealing past, and everything that has come to light about his relationship with Jessica, all the way back to when she was a minor, the entire community has turned against him overnight. Annie did a first-class job of spreading the lurid details throughout the neighborhood. The news she called me with this morning is exactly what I was hoping to hear— the community center held an emergency board meeting and voted unanimously to remove Rick from his position as youth program director effective immediately. Lynn West's life is rapidly crumbling on all fronts.

"I suspect the youth program will struggle to make it now that it's been blacklisted by a scandal of such magnitude,"

Annie muses. "People are understandably reluctant to send their children to these kinds of programs where predators have easy access to them. And social services will be reticent about allowing foster children to attend after what happened to Jessica, given that she was in the system at the time."

I make a noise at the back of my throat to express my disgust. "It gives me the creeps to think I was living next door to a predator. I'm telling you what, Annie, my life has been a nightmare ever since the story broke. I disconnected my doorbell, but I've had reporters banging on my front door at all hours, slipping requests for an exclusive under the mat and in my letterbox."

"That's terrible, dear. Can't the police do anything to stop them?"

"No, but I talked to my landlord this morning, and he's agreed to dissolve my rental contract, under the circumstances. I don't want to deal with this kind of harassment. It could go on for a long time. Fortunately, I can run my online business from anywhere. It's best if I move away and start over."

"But you only just got here a few months ago," Annie protests.

"I know, but something like this leaves a bad taste in your mouth. I'm not comfortable living here anymore." I let out a weary sigh. "I'm just so worried about Jessica and the baby."

"Charles is convinced the police will get to the bottom of it before too long. If Rick has harmed them, he'll face the full extent of the law," Annie reassures me. "When are you planning on moving?"

"Some time in the next day or two. As soon as I've packed up all my inventory."

"We'll certainly miss having you in the neighborhood. I've enjoyed our tea and chats. And Daisy will miss her walks with you. Make sure and send me your new address so we can stay in touch. Will you keep your phone number?"

"Yes, of course," I reply, smiling to myself as I lie through my teeth. Annie will never hear from me again. In another day or so, Nora Munroe and *Raven Streetwear* will cease to exist.

I break the news to Charles later on that afternoon when I pick up Daisy for our farewell walk together. He looks thoughtful but doesn't seem overly surprised. He probably saw this coming—he knows firsthand how stressful this entire situation has been for me. "Where are you relocating to?"

"Michigan," I say without hesitation. "It's not too far from my supplier, so overnight shipping shouldn't be a problem."

I've never been to Michigan, and I won't be going there next week either. I'm actually meeting Jessica in Canton to pick up my baby. And after that, I plan on driving straight to New York where Jonathan and I will disappear among the masses.

38

NOVEMBER 21, 2008

I'm dragging my heels—pretending to agonize over assets I couldn't care less about—and my attorney's growing impatient with me. I'm back to questioning if divorce is really the right course of action. Would it be better for our son if we stay together, give it some more time at least? I'm torn between not wanting to leave you but needing to protect Jonathan. I guess I don't want to give up hope that you'll turn a corner any day now. Stupid, I know, considering how many times you've lied to me in the past. I don't want our son to grow up with this much conflict in the home, but then divorce is hard on kids too.

It drives a stake through my heart every time I think about how I'll have to sit down with Jonathan one day and justify why I broke up our family unit. Although really, you're the one who instigated it and left me to pick up the pieces. I'll have to explain to our son what addiction is and what it does to a person, and the dangers you exposed us to. Surely you must realize you're putting us at risk. Associating with shady types, engaging in criminal activity. What if someone follows you home one night? I've even lain awake worrying that the police might raid the house. I'm pretty sure you're not dealing, but then I didn't think you were using either. So

I could be flat wrong about that too. I don't even think the police need a warrant if they're going to arrest you.

Can you imagine how traumatized our son would be if they stormed the house and hauled you off in handcuffs? I might end up facing criminal charges if they find a large enough quantity of drugs in the house. They could claim I was complicit and seize our assets. I've been reading up on civil asset forfeiture cases and it's frightening what happens to people. How would I ever be able to hold my head up in public again if the police conduct a drug raid at our house? It's not a great way to make friends at preschool either. Don't forget we signed Jonathan up to start next fall at Little Creek.

He's too young to understand what's going on yet, but I'm sure he's picking up on all the tension. I'm scared he might be predisposed to addiction too. That's another reason I have to get him away from you. I need to stick to my decision to seek a divorce. I'll find a way to tell you tonight. No more waffling. I only hope our son doesn't blame me one day for tearing his family apart before he had a chance to make any lasting memories with us. I hope he understands that I did it for him, that I was saving him, even though I couldn't save you.

39

PRESENT DAY

My heart burns with feverish anticipation as I near the Plaza Court Motel where I've arranged to meet Jessica. It's hard to believe a woman would be willing to part with her own flesh and blood. But I know druggies better than most. For the right amount of money, they will do virtually anything. And I offered Jessica a tidy sum, double what the Wests were offering, which should be more than enough to feed her addiction for several years to come. Not that I really have that kind of money to give her. I pat the inner pocket of my coat. But I do have a little something for her—enough of a supply for her to shoot up for a couple of days in this sleazy motel I booked her into, by which time I'll be long gone with Jonathan. Finally, he'll be safe from all the dangerous people in his world.

As I pull into the Plaza Court Motel parking lot, I can't help but shudder at the sight. The exterior is peeling and faded, giving the impression it is as weary of life as its occupants. Several of the bulbs in the neon sign have burned out and others flicker to life intermittently. The sooner I get Jonathan out of this dive, the better. It's not a healthy environment for children. It's the sort of place where all manner of illegal transactions are conducted, and the rooms are probably full of mold and every kind of human germ. Glancing at the text from Jessica on my phone, I double check the room number she gave me—107. Smart choice. I remember how hard it is navigating stairs with a newborn. Some memories have stuck, others have blurred with time. I crawl at five miles per hour past a row of curtained windows, behind which televisions glimmer and blare, until I reach Jessica's room.

After pulling into the nearest parking space, I turn off the engine and sink back against the seat to gather my thoughts. Everything has come together perfectly thanks to my meticulous planning. I've packed carefully for this last vital phase and the long trip ahead. The infant seat is safely installed in the center position in the back seat, a tether anchor securing it to the floor. A fully stocked diaper bag and insulated cooler filled with formula sit on the passenger seat next to me. I've checked the contents a thousand times if I've checked them once, fearful I might have forgotten something important. After all, it's been a while since I've cared for a newborn, and my memories are fragmented. I blame the medication for a lot of my confusion, which is another reason I quit taking it.

I lock my car before walking up the cracked concrete pathway to Jessica's room and rapping my knuckles on the decrepit metal door. Random initials, gang signs, and vulgar curse words are etched all over it. The number seven hanging askew on a broken nail gives up the ghost and lands at my feet. I kick it aside, my pulse racing as I hear footsteps approaching from within.

I'm sweating profusely, barely able to contain my excitement at the thought of holding a baby in my arms once more. The door swings inward with a sudden whoosh. I take a step forward and hesitate, blinking rapidly as my brain misfires, trying to compute the disconcerting scene in front of me.

"Come in, Sylvia." The unexpected sound of Doctor Miller's voice washes over me as he beckons me inside. He's using that familiar kindergarten voice he always uses when he talks to me. My head throbs as the room spins around me. Why is he here? We don't have a session today, do we?

I stumble past him on leaden legs and stare blankly at the other man in the room—my estranged husband, Nicolas. He's perched on the edge of the bed with his elbows balanced on his thighs, head in his hands. His dirty blond hair is tufted up like he's been running his fingers through it for hours. Confusion floods my brain. Why is he sitting on Jessica's bed? Did he come here for Jonathan? My pulse thuds in my temples. I won't let him! I'll fight him. I won't let Nicolas take my baby away from me again.

"Where's Jonathan? I want to see him." My throat feels clogged as the words fall from my lips, my eyes flitting anxiously between Nicolas and Doctor Miller.

Doctor Miller adjusts his spectacles. "Jonathan's dead, Sylvia, remember?"

Sylvia … Nora … I shake my head to rid myself of the cottony feeling inside it. "No! Jessica promised him to me. She doesn't want him. And Lynn doesn't deserve him!"

"We've gone over this before, Sylvia," Doctor Miller says in an overly patient monotone.

My husband casts a tired glance my way. "You've been gone for months, Sylvia. Where were you?"

I twirl to face him, my anger mounting to uncontrollable heights. "You murdered our son!" I scream. "What are you doing here?"

"Your neighbor, Charles, tracked me down and told me what was going on," he replies. His voice sounds flat in a sad sort of way.

Is he sad because Jonathan's dead? Because he killed him? I wrack my brains trying to remember if he ever told me he was sorry. I'm swimming in hazy memories. Something is wrong with this picture, but I can't figure out what.

I rub my brow furiously. "Why did Charles call you? He was helping me and Jessica. He knew what Rick was doing to her and—"

"Charles knew what *you* were doing to her," Nicolas interrupts.

"What are you talking about?" My voice pitches to a level of hysteria I'm all too familiar with. I'm losing control. It feels as if there's a noxious gas dispersing through my head, eroding my ability to think.

"The brainwashing, the manipulation," Nicolas replies calmly. "When Charles learned you'd hinted to Annie that Jessica might disappear, he sensed something was seriously amiss. He had a long talk with Jessica last week. She told him all about your proposition to buy her baby. Charles realized you were unstable, Nora. He's worked with enough mentally ill people in his day to recognize the telltale signs."

I'm beginning to hyperventilate. That dopehead Jessica sold me out. "What else did Charles tell you?" I hiss at my husband.

Nicolas rubs a hand across his chin. "He figured out that you were trying to set Rick up after you pretended Daisy had discovered something buried in his backyard. Charles did some investigating and found out from Jeff that you'd also gone into Rick's office shortly before the police found the card signed by Jessica. And Lynn told him Jessica misplaced her laptop—the same laptop that conveniently turned up with all those incriminating diary entries when the police searched her flat. It wasn't hard for an old hand like Charles to put two and two together."

My shoulders begin to shake. A cold fear grips my bones.

My plan has been derailed. I'm not going to drive away from the Plaza Court Motel with my baby strapped in that brand-new car seat after all. "Where is he?" I rasp. "Where's Jonathan?"

Nicolas shoots a quick glance at Doctor Miller. "He's safe. Jessica is giving her baby up for adoption, like she wanted to do all along."

I turn to Doctor Miller, a serpent-like fear uncoiling in my gut. "Why are you here?"

He clears his throat. "Charles ran a background check on you and decided to contact me first before alerting the police. I explained to him that you had stopped taking your medication and that you were a broken woman, driven to do what you did by the depth of your grief. Charles was very understanding of the extenuating circumstances, and he agreed to help me stage an intervention. We can end this now if you consent to come with me and resume in-house treatment."

I stare at the stained, herringbone carpet, random thoughts firing in quick succession through my brain. I am a broken woman, broken by grief. I remember Doctor Miller telling me that in one of our sessions after my release. He said I was broken, but that I could get better if I really wanted to. I thought I did. Maybe I still do. I want the pain to go away.

I massage my throbbing forehead, squinting across the room at my estranged husband. It's all coming back to me now. I remember why Lynn West advocated for him. My throat begins to close over as a sickening realization envelops me like a sticky web from which I can't escape.

Nicolas didn't kill our son. He wasn't driving the car high on amphetamines the night Jonathan and Bella died.

It was me.

CHAPTER 40

PRESENT DAY

I don't know why I felt the urge to go down to the basement and look for this old journal. Maybe it was something Doctor Miller said, "Jonathan's dead, Sylvia, remember?" Did you really think you could replace our son by taking someone else's baby?

All of a sudden, I had this intense longing to remember how I felt in the months leading up to his death. The pain, the confusion, frustration, anger, despair. I stopped writing in my journal the night of the crash. I just couldn't do it anymore, even though my therapy group told me it was more important than ever to keep journaling. But I couldn't see the point. Yes, it was partly therapeutic for me, but it was mostly a record for Jonathan, to help him understand why I made the decision to leave you. Now he'll never read it.

Two police officers came to the door the night of the accident to break the news to me. One fresh-faced novice, lips twitching nervously as he stammered a greeting, the other a veteran at monotone delivery of life-altering news. It's still surreal thinking back to that moment. Unimaginable terror gripped me. It felt as if my insides were being stretched out across an expanse as wide as the heavens. In an instant, my heart shattered into a million tiny pieces. People talk about grief leaving you feeling empty inside, but I didn't feel empty at the time. I was full of heartbreak and loss and love—so full it physically hurt.

Everything I did was for nothing. All I ever wanted was a better future for our son. I was so careful never to leave you alone with Jonathan after the night you fell asleep all drugged up on the couch and let him wander outside on his own. I'll always be grateful to Bella for staying by his side. I still believe she kept him safe in the back yard. Not that it made any difference in the end.

I was fast asleep that night. I didn't hear you take the car and leave. I can't help blaming myself for what happened to some extent. At group, they always used to tell me not to do that. But I still find myself going over and over it all in my mind. Retracing my steps in some misguided attempt to figure out where I went wrong. If I hadn't threatened to leave you, if I hadn't served you with divorce papers, if I hadn't filed for custody, maybe I wouldn't have driven you over the edge. Maybe you wouldn't have felt so desperate, so trapped, and you wouldn't have tried to flee with Jonathan. You wouldn't have crashed the car high on Adderall. Our son would still be alive.

I didn't know how to help you out of the pit you fell into after-ward. PTSD and severe depression. You were paranoid and confused, convinced someone else had killed Jonathan. I wasn't sure at first if they would send you to prison or to an institution. I figured it didn't matter either way. The irony was that you were finally going to get the help you needed. You'd be forced to detox cold turkey. Too little too late to save our son.

Even then, I never stopped loving you, Sylvia. I promised you that when you got out, I would be waiting for you if you wanted to come back home. But you still can't accept what you did. I don't think you ever will.

Your loving husband,
Nicolas

I KNOW WHAT YOU DID

Ready for another suspense-filled read with shocking plot twists and turns along the way? Check out my psychological thriller *I Know What You Did* on Amazon!

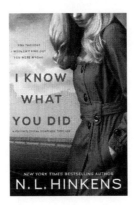

She only took what she deserved. She never expected what happened next.

After suffering multiple miscarriages, school counselor Jo Murphy is on a mission to save her marriage by any means possible. When Mia, a pregnant senior, unexpectedly shows up in her office, Jo devises an unorthodox plan to adopt her baby. But Mia's boyfriend suddenly goes missing, and the investigation that follows unearths one shocking secret after another until all at once nothing about Mia is adding up. Trapped in a web of deceit of her own making, Jo finds herself embroiled in a heart-stopping murder plot that threatens to destroy the one thing she wants most.

What if her baby's mother is a killer?

- An emotional roller coaster of a domestic thriller that will leave you breathless! -

---

Do you enjoy reading across genres? I also write young adult science fiction and fantasy thrillers. You can find out more about those titles at www.normahinkens.com. *Turn the page and read on to enjoy two bonus science fiction thriller stories to whet your appetite!*

A QUICK FAVOR

Dear Reader,

I hope you enjoyed reading *The Silent Surrogate* as much as I enjoyed writing it. Thank you for taking the time to check out my books and I would appreciate it from the bottom of my heart if you would leave a review, long or short, on Amazon as it makes a HUGE difference in helping new readers find the series.

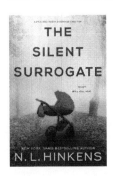

To be the first to hear about my upcoming book releases, sales, and fun giveaways, jump on board my VIP Reader Club at www.normahinkens.com and follow me on Twitter, Instagram and Facebook. Feel free to email me at norma@normahinkens.com with any feedback or comments. I LOVE hearing from readers. YOU are the reason I keep going through the tough times.

All my best,
Norma

WHEN I FIND YOU

A SCIENCE FICTION THRILLER STORY

Erratic gusts of a cold solar wind slash my face as I steer my way past the queue of refugees coiled around Percuto's Migration Ministry building. Some shoot angry glares my way, and I paste on what I hope passes for an apologetic smile as I scan my wrist chip at the gate and log in at 5:07 a.m. They've been waiting here for days, but I have an illegally downloaded migration appointment. If they knew why, they would willingly give up their place in line for me.

"So many," I say to the guard monitoring the scanner.

"Take the free land on the frontier planets, take your chances," she grumbles as she waves me through to join an even longer line inside the fence.

"They wanted to farm. Not fight a war," I say, keeping my tone neutral.

"They traded citizenship for land," the guard replies, her tone as frosty as her expression. "Not our job to get them to the Inner Ring now." She turns her back on me and gives a disgruntled wave to the next person in line.

During last week's inter-planetary summit, Galactic Guerrillas bombed a government building on Kwan, the largest of the frontier planets. The Supreme Leader's response was swift. Anarchy followed, which is why the settlers have been flooding back here to the tiny spaceport of Percuto, the gateway to the Inner Ring, Under the protection of the Galactic Migration Treaty, they have one week to secure passage on a transit ship out of here, or face deportation back to the frontier planets. My heart breaks for them, but I need to bide my time.

A cyborg with a megaphone mounted in his forehead, patrols the crowd outside the gate, barking an unrelenting sequence of instructions in PremierTalk, the official language of the Inner Ring. His foul mood is a good indication he was ordered here against his will to help coordinate the refugee crisis.

"Seeeengle file only--migration exit interviews only!" he bellows.

"What does he think we're here for? Lava facials?" I whisper to the teenager in front of me. She frowns, flicks her long, blond hair over her shoulder and shakes her head vehemently by way of response. Maybe she thinks it's bad juju to be seen conversing with the other applicants before her exit interview. Only a few transit ships are permitted to fly to the Inner Ring each week. And there are only so many spots on board.

I'm not supposed to be interacting with the other applicants anyway according to Sanya, the operative who trained me. "No casual conversations," she warned me. "People remember things."

With a shrug, I pull out my holographic tablet and concentrate on channeling out the crabby cyborg.

Three-and-a-half hours later, I reach the heavily-guarded entryway to the Migration Ministry building. Armed cyborgs rummage through our belongings and divest us of our outerwear before they allow us inside. Shepherded in batches of twenty, we pass through the jaws of a steel elevator. An overwhelming stench of body odor rises as we descend. Fear melding with exhaustion. My stomach churns, but Sanya's words prevail—"Don't attract attention."

The elevator jerks, then shudders to a stop. The doors retract, and I recoil at the pockmarked face of the female officer who signals us out with a spastic jerk of a pudgy thumb and a strange clicking sound. The sulky blonde who shut me down earlier glances at me uncertainly. With a roll of my eyes, I step past her and follow our escort as she schleps along a windowless corridor. Jobs in the Migration Ministry are undesirable to Inner Ring citizens; short of cyborgs, she's probably all they could muster. If she only knew how some of us are forced to make a living.

When we enter the processing waiting room, the migration officer slams down a tablet full of case files in front of the small glass window of an enclosed booth. A metal claw slides out with a loud clank and retrieves it.

"Commit every detail to memory," Sanya said when she gave me my new identity. I did. Deception comes easy to me. Especially after everything I've had to do to survive.

We worked together for months on extensive language retraining. "One word, and a good linguist can nail you," Sanya stressed many times. I have no trace of an accent now. No apparent ties to the indentured past my father sold me into after he sent my mother to a penal colony on the fringe, along with the other concubines he banished. She died there six weeks later. I should be dead too--indentured children don't usually survive the brutality of their masters more than a few months. And most don't escape. Turns out I'm good at a lot of things, but that's not the real reason the Guerrillas sought me out.

I scope the stale, white-walled room bedecked with

Galactic flags from every sovereign nation in the frontier. Percuton citizens are packed into tight rows on blue metal benches floating up from the floor. Their eyes bore into us as we take our seats. Every new arrival is a threat to their chance of securing passage out of here today.

I'm careful not to look directly at the cameras, scowling down on us from their vantage point above bleached out prints of Last Station Moon and the Solar Overpass. Laser resculpting has dramatically altered my appearance, aged me even, but cameras can reverse engineer such procedures if they detect an anomaly. I hastily gulp back the bile rising up my throat. The last thing I need is a medical droid doing a trace on my DNA.

Thanks to Sanya's connections in the dark interstellar-sphere, I'm registered as an employee of a reputable commercial design firm. My records indicate that I travel to the Inner Ring regularly for work. I suppress a grin. Maybe I could offer the dilapidated Migration Ministry building a makeover, kick start my new career.

"You're all stuck here in this room for as long as it takes so don't gripe about it," the pockmarked migration officer barks at us from the front of the room. She leans a blubbery forearm on a podium draped with Inner Ring flag bunting, flanked on either side by a a potted Orb Snap tree and a large statue of the Supreme Leader of the Inner Ring. I shudder when I stare into the statue's unmoving eyes. Those eyes have haunted me for years.

Another migration officer behind the glass window leans into the microphone. "Zola Gainstorm, proceed to the front of the room." A few rows in front of me Gainstorm gets to her feet. She totters across the tile in spiked heels, her plunging neckline cataloging her assets.

A tall, elderly woman with a kink in her neck appears in the doorway clutching a tablet. She's dressed in the ivory uniform that all officials of the Inner Ring wear. She peers down at Gainstorm with an air of disdain. The plunging neckline isn't likely to swing the vote in this case, although there are no shortage of migration officers willing to take bribes of one kind or another. A few hundred credits secured my appointment.

The officer disappears with Gainstorm, and I steal a glance to my left. A heavyset woman at the end of my row is trying too hard to make a statement of another kind. She glitters like a patriotic ornament in her red and white striped skirt and matching headscarf with holographic Inner Ring flags that sparkle every time she moves. To my horror, she arches an aggressively waxed brow at me and crosses her forefingers in a rebel gesture.

I quickly turn my head, my pulse racing. Surely she can't have recognized me. I suck in a breath between my teeth, willing myself to stay calm. It's not possible. Instinctively, I pull my sleeve down over my wrist, even though Sanya's surgical team has long since removed the tattoo marking me as a convict.

Sanya secured my early release from the reform colony. She told me the Galactic Guerrillas had been looking for me for a long time. And then she told me I had the power to end their struggle, and mine. Hatred is a powerful motivator; it bonds Sanya and I, defines what we do. But in the end, I must act alone.

I suck at the rank air and glance around our sweatbox. The intelligent-looking man on my right strokes his chin, writing in spurts on his tablet.

"Quite the novel you have going there," I remark, breaking Sanya's cardinal rule for the second time.

He chuckles. "I regret I am but a humble journalist in pursuit of truth." His eyes pierce mine. "And what, may I ask, are you in pursuit of?"

I give a stilted smile. "The Inner Ring dream, of course." My heart races and I turn away. I casually tuck a strand of transplanted chestnut hair behind my ear. The procedure hurt more than I thought it would, but I'd sacrifice anything for this mission to succeed. Dying my blond hair wouldn't have sufficed; the Minders' scanners could detect the anomaly if I were intercepted for any reason.

Sensing the journalist's eyes on me, I pull out my holographic tablet and pretend to be absorbed in my work. He'll have plenty to write about twenty-four hours from now, if our mission succeeds.

At 4:05 p.m. they call my name. I stand and walk to the end of the row, then make my way to the front of the room. I look around expecting the migration officer with the kink in her neck, but she's nowhere to be seen. Unsure where I'm supposed to go, I pivot between the podium and the long-departed Orb Snap tree. Two gray suits appear and scan the space with implanted bio-readout lenses. Intergalactic Intelligence Officers. My stomach plummets.

"Memorize their names and faces," Sanya told me repeatedly. *Olark Ivalch and Dajar Bartan.* I even know their kids' birthdays. I watch as they begin a synchronized stride down the room and stop at the row where the heavyset woman in the sparkly holographic headscarf is seated. Silently, I release a shaky breath. They're not here for me this time.

"Nilcha Evrork, under the terms of the Galactic Anti-Guerilla Act, you are hereby under arrest for alleged involvement in terrorist activity on the frontier planets."

I'm forgotten, left standing in front of the statue of the Supreme Leader, his frozen gaze skewering me like he knows who the real threat is. I squeeze my fists at my sides as the Intelligence Officers place a stun-brace around the woman's neck. There's nothing I can do to help her that won't mean sacrificing the mission.

In a final act of rebellion, she yanks the headscarf from her head, tosses it to the floor and stamps on it before breaking into a rousing rendition of the Galactic Guerrillas anthem. One of the suits activates the stun-brace, and the woman crumples like a discarded rag.

The pockmarked migration officer glares around the room, hands straddling her generous hips. She shuffles back behind her podium and slaps it hard. "One rotten rebel! Just takes one rotten rebel to mess up the transit," she preaches.

The other migration applicants gawk like startled prey, no doubt wondering if they're all under arrest. The Inner Ring headscarf glitters like a strobe light from the floor; the journalist's sweaty face glistening under its holographic gleam. His pen tap-dances across the page, doubtless drafting some clever headline.

When the suits drag the woman from the room, the elderly officer with the kink in her neck reappears. She looks me up and down, her black-eyed gaze grim. "Riverienne Bosneck?"

I give a deferential nod to my new identity.

"This way." The officer turns and lopes off down a narrow corridor. I take a calming breath and follow several feet behind her, counting steps and memorizing doorways as we go by. An ingrained habit. Always prepare for the getaway. Finally, she halts outside a room and gestures for me to go inside. I hesitate when I see the neuro-hub in the center of the room. Despite all the training for this moment, it doesn't make it any less intimidating. The reconstituted sausage I ate for breakfast churns in my stomach.

"You can take a seat and relax for a few minutes while I calibrate the machine," the officer says, following me inside. She makes her way across to a control panel and leans over it. From behind I see her neck juts out at an odd angle and I wonder why she hasn't had it surgically corrected in the Inner

Ring. Maybe she can't afford it. It fits with my suspicion that Migration Ministry positions are punitive rather than paid.

"Almost ready," the officer says, glancing up. "I just need to confirm your answers to a few basic questions. Please state your name for the record."

Mirelda Iyak. I lean back against the headrest designed to hold me in position while my brainwaves are analyzed. "Riverienne Bosneck."

"Age and IQ?"

"Twenty-seven, 243."

I'm actually only seventeen, too young to qualify for unaccompanied migration, but my records were easy to falsify in the dark interstellarsphere. My IQ is another matter. I can't hide it. The neuro-hub will take an accurate reading once it links with my brain. Thankfully it will be a favorable mark on my application.

"And your current occupation?"

Undercover operative for the Galactic Guerrillas. "Commercial designer for SpaceStellar Originals," I reply.

"All right, that should do it." The officer seems satisfied with my answers and even flicks me a smile as she tilts my head and lowers the brain scanner over my skull. I eye her long fingernails, painted a pearlescent silver the exact shade of the scanner. I wonder if it's a regulation color, just like her ivory uniform.

"Authentication of your migration application should only take a few minutes," she says. "First, I'll need to do a routine test of your blood to rule out the presence of any neuro-inhibiting substances."

"Of course," I say, rolling up my sleeve.

She pricks me with a plasma extractor and glances at the result. "Excellent, let's begin." She turns her back on me and retreats to the control station.

With a flick of my tongue, I release the neuroinhibitor from the implanted fake molar on the left side of my mouth. I lean back and close my eyes. The room is strangely calm and the air is cool against my forehead, unlike the claustrophobic waiting room.

My limbs relax as colors and words slowly merge together in a kaleidoscope of patterns. My head spins, but I can't say for sure if I'm falling or flying. Flashes of thought rush through my head and scramble like a crossword before I can process them. The statue's cold eyes zero in on me. *When I find you ...*

Sanya's face flutters past me multiple times like a holographic chain. *Trust the process. Don't fight the images.* Her voice ripples like water, calming me as the neuro-hub's sensors probe deep inside my brain. I've run through this drill a thousand times and passed the screening ninety-eight percent of the time. But it's never a given.

"And that completes the screening interview," the migration officer says, her gleaming fingernails scraping my forehead as she pulls the brain scanner away from my head. I blink open my eyes and give a dazed nod.

"You can pick up your migration authentication two doors down on the right. A guard will escort you to the transit ship."

Silently, I repeat her words to myself to be sure of their meaning. *I'm approved.* Relief and exhilaration surge through my veins as I get to my feet. I'm on my way to the Inner Ring at last.

***

As soon as I disembark from the transit ship in the bustling Inner Ring docking station, I spot my holographic name displayed above a driverless Hoverped. *Riverienne Bosneck.* I allow myself a wry grin as I climb aboard. If only the Supreme Leader knew who had really just arrived in the Inner Ring.

A tinted windshell closes down over me sealing out the clamor and hiding me from sight. Armed droids patrol the perimeter of the station, scanning the crowd for anomalies. My readout won't show any signs of heightened stress; even the sweat glands in my armpits have been removed by the surgeons. Only my thudding heartbeat betrays the fact that I'm hiding secrets. One deadly secret.

The Hoverped exits the station without incident and delivers me to a nondescript motel in a seedy part of town. The windshell opens back up and I dismount with trepidation. It's dusk, and the street is unlit. All at once I'm unsure if the Hoverped is really part of Sanya's plan or if I've been intercepted by Minders and brought here for interrogation, or worse. The handful of people trawling the streets keep their eyes fixed on the ground in front of them as they walk. The air hangs thick with an odor of rot, and sepia-colored insects circle the trash heaped up next to an overflowing dumpster. I glance furtively up and down the grungy line of doorways leading into unidentifiable businesses, desperately searching for any sign of Sanya.

A passerby lifts his head and throws me a sidelong glance. His face is seared with ridges, like a piece of grilled meat, and his bloodshot eyes are veined. I startle when he beams a hologram onto the curb at my feet before vanishing down an alleyway. *Room 246.* Sanya must be waiting for me inside. A foreboding tingle goes through me as the image fades before my eyes. Sanya never leaves a trail to follow. And this mission has no margin of error.

My stomach muscles tighten as I approach the retractable door of the motel and enter the dingy lobby. I nod in the direction of the cyborg concierge fixated on a telescreen at the reception counter and take the elevator to the second floor. The deserted corridor is even darker than the lobby, lit only by a ghoulish recessed lamp. I knock twice on the door of room 246, wait for a reciprocal double rap and then knock twice again. I chew on my bottom lip until the door swings wide. Sanya's eyes light up with approval, but she doesn't crack a smile. I'm not sure she knows how.

"About time you showed your face," I blurt out. "I was beginning to think it was Minders who had picked me up."

"They don't conduct interrogations in motels," she says, in a guarded tone.

I throw a withering look around the room. "You picked a sleazy one to meet in."

Sanya arches a sculpted brow. "How was your trip?"

"The transit was uneventful, but the Migration Processing Ministry was sketchy."

Sanya frowns. "Did something happen?"

I shrug. "Not to me. A rebel from one of the frontier planets was arrested."

"You didn't converse with her at all, did you?"

I shake my head.

"Good. It shouldn't be a problem." Sanya turns and reaches behind her for a dark gray pack. "Your uniform is hanging in the closet. Everything else you'll need for the job is in here. SpaceStellar Originals is scheduled to finish up work on the Supreme Leader's offices tomorrow. You will meet with him at noon to do a final inspection of the work. A company vehicle will pick you up here at seven-thirty sharp."

"Will you be in it?'

"I don't work for Interstellar. That's your cover," she says, checking the contents of the pack. She scrutinizes me for a moment. "If my schedule allows, we may see each other in the morning."

"How will I signal our contact?"

"Once you are safely in the vehicle you will be provided with everything you need."

I grab the bag she hands to me without looking at it. "And afterward? Do I get another ride on a driverless Hoverped out of here?"

Sanya's brow wrinkles as if she hasn't even considered the possibility there will be an afterward. It doesn't do much to reassure me of our chances.

"Of course," she says, briskly. "You will be relocated to another quadrant in the Inner Ring." She hesitates and clears her throat. "We will operate from there until the situation has … stabilized."

Before I can ask another question, she turns on her heel and disappears out the door. I turn and toss the bag on the shabby bed floating out from the wall. I'm assuming this is where I'm to spend the night.

Sleep eludes me, although I doze for a few minutes here and there. The weight of the task ahead lies heavy on me. If I fail tomorrow, the Guerrillas will face a long and bloody struggle to overthrow the Supreme Leader and his iron-fisted Inner Ring regime. But I can change the odds. I hold the keys to the kingdom, which is why Sanya searched for me for all those years. And why I'm about to singlehandedly pull off a coup … or die trying.

When a milky dawn finally filters through the cracks in the shutters on my window, I roll out of bed and traipse into the grimy adjoining bathroom. Five minutes later, dressed in a charcoal-colored SpaceStellar Originals uniform, I head downstairs to the lobby. "Where can I get some breakfast?" I ask the cyborg at the front desk.

She glances up, a bored look in her one eye, and points a steel finger down the hallway. "Second door on your left. Seat yourself."

My stomach rumbles as I make my way to the dining

room. I haven't eaten in over twenty-four hours, and this could turn out to be the last meal of the condemned, so I intend to make it count.

There's only one other patron inside, an elderly man in a black overcoat hunched over a table in the corner. I ignore him and head straight for the buffet dispenser. The menu is bleak--no meat or fruit--but I'm willing to eat almost anything at this point. I select a plate of eggs and a muffin, along with a mug of coffee. A moment later, a steel flap swings up and my plate appears on a conveyor belt. Minus the muffin. *Great.* I reach for the unappetizing arrangement of eggs, grab my coffee, and head over to a table by the door. I jab my fork into the congealed eggs and chew a mouthful. Reconstituted, but at least it's protein, and I'll need all the energy I can get.

"Rubbery, ain't it?" a raspy voice says.

My head shoots up and my heart jolts in my chest. *The elderly man in the overcoat.* I berate myself for not hearing him approach. I swallow my food in one painful gulp. A wad of egg lodges in my throat and I take a swig of lukewarm coffee.

"You're not from these parts, are you?" he asks.

"Are you?" I ask coldly.

He vacuums a wad of saliva through a gap in his teeth as he appraises me.

I recoil, bracing for a Minder stun-gun, but instead he leans toward me.

"I'm from wherever Sanya says I'm from," he whispers.

I frown and throw a furtive glance out into the hallway, but there's no sign of the cyborg. "There are ears every-where," I mouth back to him.

"And my job's to weed them out," he says, straightening up. "Change of plan. Your ride's out back." He turns up the collar of his overcoat and strides out of the room with a brisk gait that doesn't match the age lines in his face.

My pulse is pounding in my temples. He must be one of us. How else would he know about Sanya? I glance up at the holographic display on the wall. The vehicle's early. A flicker of apprehension goes through me. I hurriedly push my plate aside, gather up my bags and make my way to the back of the motel.

A sleek, bullet-shaped vehicle is parked at the curb. I quickly scan up and down the street for any sign of Minders before heading outside. A retractable door glides up into the roof, and I climb inside clutching the gray pack Sanya gave me. I still haven't looked in it because I already know what it contains. A scalpel, a chip extractor and a sterile implanter. Tools of the trade. My job at the penal colony was to extract dead prisoners' chips for recycling. I learned to do it quickly and efficiently, even by touch with my eyes closed when the sight became too overwhelming. This will be more difficult. The tools are polyethylene prototypes, hidden in the barrel of a fake hairbrush.

The company vehicle whips through increasingly opulent districts bustling with sculpted people, their faces a startling combination of flawless and vacant. I straighten up when we reach a remotely manned checkpoint. Rapid-fire antimatter lasers target our vehicle until we're cleared to pass into the Inner Ring government district. We pull up outside a sleek, charcoal-tinted glass building that soars upward for several hundred meters. I wait for the vehicle's retractable door to open, but instead, a compartment on my left slides open revealing a tablet.

"Activate the TransferTablet when you are ready to accept payment," an electronic voice chimes out.

I shake my head in disbelief. Sanya has a nerve if she really intends to collect payment on this job. And then it hits me. Activating the tablet will alert our contact in the dark interstellarsphere. I grab the tablet and stuff it into the gray pack, then put on my solar shades before exiting the vehicle.

Sanya is waiting for me on the sidewalk. My mouth almost falls open, but I catch myself in time. She's dressed in the ivory uniform of Inner Ring government officials. Which explains how she moves around so freely. A twinge of doubt goes through my mind, but I dismiss it. She has no reason to double cross me. Her parents died in a liquidation camp. She hates the Supreme Leader almost as much as I do.

She steps forward and shakes my hand for the benefit of the security cameras. "I'm Towla Wentian. I'm here to escort you to the Supreme Leader's offices for the final inspection." She hesitates and looks at me pointedly. "He asked that the meeting be brought forward."

Not trusting myself to speak, I give a curt nod to indicate I understand. If the Supreme Leader's pressed for time, it narrows my window of opportunity. I need to be ready.

The guards at the entryway direct us into a laser scanner designed to analyze our readouts and cross-reference them with criminal and fugitive databases across the galaxy. I try not to flinch when it's my turn to step inside. Even though the guards are unaware my results are being coded in from the dark interstellarsphere, I breathe out a silent sigh of relief when the light turns green, and I'm free to follow Sanya inside the building. The hack will be discovered eventually, but by then I'll either be dead or the Inner Ring will be under Guerrilla control.

We ride up the elevator to the Supreme Leader's offices in silence. Everything we say and do is being recorded inside this building. When we reach the eighteenth floor, Sanya scans her wrist chip on a keypad and the elevator doors open. "Please don't hesitate to contact me should you need any further assistance," she says, with a stiff bow. For a moment our eyes lock and I see a flash of emotion. She's counting on me. So many have died at the Supreme Leader's hand, but if I succeed today, many more lives will be spared.

I step out into the hallway and the elevator doors seal shut with a soft whoosh behind me. I wonder if I'll ever see Sanya again.

I walk toward a pair of steel doors embossed with the Inner Ring seal. A hidden camera whirs as it verifies my clearance. The doors slide soundlessly apart and I step into an opulent, gleaming space filled with floating furniture and holographic surfaces. So beautiful it takes my breath away. I wander through the room, careful not to disturb anything. Hard to believe I'm in the heart of the Inner Ring dynasty. In the offices of the Supreme Leader.

The suite is eerily silent. In the center of a plush seating arrangement, I spot an ornate two-tiered platter of plump berries surrounded by an intricate floral display on a glass table. Saliva pools beneath my tongue. I've only tasted real berries one time; in payment for a job I did. The long-forgotten memory of the sweet gushing juice on my tongue is suddenly overwhelming. I'd like nothing more than to gorge myself on the heaped platter, but I restrain myself from swiping one, even though I know I could pull it off without the cameras detecting my sleight of hand.

I continue past the seating area, and stare, dumbfounded, at the grandeur of the Supreme Leader's intricately carved white marble desk. I stretch out my fingers and run them along its smooth surface. "Stunning!" I gasp.

"Indeed," a voice booms out.

I spin around as a short, obese man shuffles into view, accompanied on either side by a military droid. His face is sculpted to an indeterminate age and his thick braided hair writhes like a hangman's rope down his back.

I bow before him, every nerve in my body tingling with loathing. It takes everything in me not to lunge forward and grab him by the neck. When I lift my head, his eyes are on me. "Sanya tells me you are the designer responsible for this magnificence?"

I bow again, not wanting to make prolonged eye contact. My implanted colored lenses don't feel adequate to hide the truth from his penetrating gaze. "It was an honor," I say, feigning awe for the man I despise more than anyone I've ever known.

He clicks his fingers and the droids retreat. I make a mental note of the stun-braces dangling from their tool belts.

The Supreme Leader gestures lavishly toward the seating arrangement. "Sit, let us talk."

"It's a beautiful arrangement," I say, motioning at the platter of berries as I take a seat next to him.

His fat lips twist in an oddly familiar smile. "Beautiful, but deadly." He plucks a berry and studies it, twisting it between his thumb and forefinger. "Hickleberries. They contain a toxin that paralyzes their hapless victim in seconds." He leans toward me conspiratorially. "I keep them here for the staff. I like to know who's stealing from me."

A shudder runs through me. For one panicked moment I imagine he knows.

Then I pull myself together.

"Loyalty should be tested," I say, with an approving smile.

He waves a fat finger in my face. "I like how you think. And I like your work. I want to discuss another project I have in mind for you, but unfortunately, I'm short on time today." He makes a dismissive gesture with his hand. "This wretched refugee situation."

"Horrendous," I say.

He glances up at a holographic time display. "Process the payment," he says. "The least I can do is make sure you're taken care of."

I blink and look away. *Make sure you're taken care of.* The

WHEN I FIND YOU

irony of his words isn't lost on me. My hand shakes as I reach into the gray pack and flick open the cap on the end of the hairbrush. My tools lie ready. I pull out the TransferTablet and activate it, and then hold it out to him. He raises his wrist to scan his embedded chip, *the chip that controls the technology for the entire Inner Ring.* I've memorized the commands I'll need to operate it. I hold the tablet steady, forcing myself not to recoil at the crepelike skin on his hand. So much older than his sculpted face appears.

Suddenly, a siren blares through the office space. The Supreme Leader hesitates, his wrist paused in mid-air.

Sanya's contact in the dark interstellarsphere has tripped the fire alarm. The building will be evacuated in minutes. The rest is up to me.

Every electrical impulse in my body activates on cue. I snatch up my tools, knowing I only have a few seconds. The droids are already bearing down on us, no doubt to evacuate us. Before the Supreme Leader grasps what's happening, I grab his wrist, and gouge out the chip in one deep slice. He lets out a spine-tingling scream and falls back on the couch, clutching his arm to his chest. Blood sprays his chin. I may have severed an artery. The unfamiliar scalpel was awkward to wield. My hand trembles as I struggle to implant the chip in my own wrist.

"Arrest her!" the Supreme Leader yells at the approaching droids. He half-lunges at me, but I'm out of his reach. With a final excruciating thrust of the implanter, I lodge the chip in position in my left wrist.

"Code 07 delete. All guards back down," I announce, holding my throbbing wrist to my mouth. I bite my lip, praying I didn't botch the command, scarcely daring to believe it will work. The Supreme Leader rocks to and fro on the couch, moaning and cursing at the droids to make haste as he nurses his wrist. His eyes widen in horror when they power down only a few feet from where he is seated. I hurry over to them and grab a stun-brace from one of their belts. The Supreme Leader struggles to hoist himself out of the couch, but I slip the stun-brace around his neck before he can make it to his feet.

His eyes dilate as he falls back against the chair, struggling to free himself with his good hand. "What do you think you're doing?" he screams, spittle dancing on his lower lip.

I take a seat beside him and flash him a scathing smile. "Disbanding the Inner Ring military for starters. Then there's the redistribution of Inner Ring property, abolition of indentureship, migration reform for non-citizens and gypsies, among other pressing Guerrilla matters to attend to."

His face pales. "Are you insane? The chip can only be activated by my DNA."

I grin as I pluck a berry from the bowl and survey it from all angles.

"Exactly!" I pop the berry into his mouth and squeeze his lips together as he struggles to spit it out. "Your DNA. The only thing you ever gave me."

I see it on his dying face. That moment when it all comes together and he knows.

I'm his bastard daughter.

THE END

Like what you just read? You might also enjoy my science fiction thriller *Girl of Fire: The Expulsion Project Book One.*

Don't forget to turn the page for your second bonus science fiction thriller story!

INTERCEPTION

A SCIENCE FICTION THRILLER STORY

When it rained the drops were black. In her seventeen years on Sutorax, Eos had never known a time when it wasn't that way. She pulled on her personal protection suit and smeared her nostrils with molecular jelly before slipping out of her apartment to meet Ligon.

Government-issued respirators were distributed free of charge to low-income families, but Eos found them unbearably clunky. She preferred to navigate the dust haze unencumbered if it remained a level five or below. She stretched her hand out in front of her and studied it. Today was a good day. She could clearly see three feet beyond the ends of her stained fingernails. Far enough to allow for a decent day's pillaging, which was how she and Ligon typically spent Solday—the only day of the week they weren't required to attend classes at the AcademPlex.

"Hey, Ligon!" Eos yelled to the tall, broad-shouldered figure hunched against the wind with his back to her.

He turned around and grinned, and Eos felt a ripple of something delicious go through her as she made her way toward him. She'd never admit to the disturbing ripple, of course. Ligon had been her best friend for as long as she could remember, and she wasn't about to jeopardize that, especially as he'd never given her any indication that his feelings for her ventured into that volatile realm beyond friendship.

Ligon was short for Ligonier, some funky small town where his parents had grown up. For a while, it had been popular among the settlers to name their children after the towns they had emigrated from back on Earth. Eos's parents, who had signed up for the colonization program as newlyweds, had bucked the trend and named her after a Greek goddess instead.

"Eos means *dawn*," her mother told her, "and you signified our new beginning."

"Earth was a ghetto back then," her father explained. "The population far outstripped the resources. Food replication factories couldn't keep up with demand."

"It was horrible! Sanitation had become an ecological crisis." Her mother shuddered in recollection. "They segregated us into boroughs and we couldn't leave unless we had a funeral pass. Only delivery drones had permits to cross the borough lines."

As young scientists, Eos's parents had been wowed by the central government's dazzling marketing campaign touting the long list of benefits available to early settlers in the colonization ring—a chain of planets discovered to be habitable back in 2089. Free housing, land, unlimited resources, and well-paying research jobs topped the bill. More importantly, no population-control restrictions.

"It didn't work out as we'd hoped," her father admitted, his voice breaking off into a disconcerting cough. "We never anticipated the dust clouds when we signed the contract agreeing to relinquish our right to return to Earth."

The dust clouds that originated from the dormant lava plains in central Sutorax were blamed for everything—from widespread infertility among the settlers, to the numerous respiratory ailments that plagued them. To make matters worse, the research fund that supported the colony had been slashed to a quarter of its original amount. Eos's parents were struggling to make ends meet.

"So, what are we hunting today?" Ligon asked, draping a cheeky grin across his handsome, freckled face.

Eos grimaced, debating their few options. "Hunting" consisted of scavenging from the dumpsters at the backs of businesses, restoring or recycling the items they found, and reselling them at the outdoor market. But pickings had been lean lately. As the settlers spread south, developing more land for agriculture, the dust clouds had worsened, and more and more people were falling on hard times.

"I'm tired of risking my neck for a few measly credits," Eos said. "Time to step up our game."

Ligon drew his rugged chestnut brows together, his expression circumspect. "What are you suggesting?"

"Let's try foraging on the military base."

Ligon snorted. "In a restricted zone? That's the dumbest idea you've had since last Solday when you talked me into rummaging around in putrid produce. I stank all week!"

Eos pinned him with a determined gaze.

"Don't look at me like that! If we're caught, we'll be kicked out of the AcademPlex, possibly deported."

"Which is exactly why no one else scavenges on the base," Eos retorted, arching a brow at him. "We could make a killing from the scrap metal in those dumpsters."

Ligon hesitated. Eos saw the longing in his eyes. He had been helping support his family ever since his father died from lung cancer last spring. His younger sister, Marfa, was crippled with respiratory ailments, and the extra money would offer the possibility of medication as well as food this month. It was all their mother could do to put a daily meal on the table.

The military base had been part of the package offered to the original settlers for their peace of mind. Two Dreadnoughts monitored Sutorox's airspace, and drones from the base regularly patrolled the impenetrable upland jungle-like uplands that carpeted the southern hemisphere of Sutorax.

But, the military remained tight-lipped about its reconnaissance missions. As far as Eos or anyone else knew, the drones monitored seismic readings and dust levels, although these alerts hardly mattered as the dust followed them everywhere.

"Come on, Ligon," Eos pressed. "Marfa needs the medication. Your mother is at her wits' end. Think of the relief it would give her to have a few extra credits." She gave him a rueful grin. "And it's my mother's birthday next week. I want to get her a real present, for once."

Ligon gave a resigned sigh. "All right, we'll scout it out. But if it looks the least bit sketchy, I'm bailing."

"Don't worry, there are no cameras by the dumpsters." Eos winked brazenly at him. "And luckily, there's a hole in the fence behind the warehouse big enough for us to slip through."

Ligon smoothed his hands over the hood of his protection suit, frowning in puzzlement. "And how would you know that?"

She shrugged. "I might have been working on it."

Ligon laughed, his leafy-green eyes crinkling up in a way that made Eos's heart beat a little faster. "Should have known this was a set up," he said. "Lead the way."

Hidden in the shadows behind the base warehouse, Eos and

Ligon worked swiftly and efficiently, sorting through the scrap metal and discarded parts, loading anything salvageable and small enough to transport in their oversized backpacks. They had become adept at assessing what fetched a reasonable return for their trouble at the market. The vendors liked them because they were good at sourcing special requests—they had been at this longer than the other kids.

When they'd amassed all they could reasonably carry between them, they flattened themselves against the side of the warehouse and began making their way back to the hole in the perimeter fence.

Voices drifting around the corner stopped them in their tracks.

"Guards!" Eos mouthed to Ligon.

He gave a curt nod and tried the handle on the nearest access door into the warehouse. Miraculously, it opened. He grabbed Eos by the sleeve of her protection suit and pulled her inside after him.

Eos barely had time to blink around the dimly-lit space before the rolling steel doors to the loading bay began to whir. "Over here!" she whispered, diving behind a nearby crate.

They hunkered down, trembling, as the automatic doors to the warehouse rolled up and two sets of dust-coated boots filed through. Eos sucked in her breath when Admiral Rice's stocky form came into view.

"It was the largest sighting to date in the upland forests, sir," the officer accompanying him said. "We marked the footage classified."

"Run it!" Admiral Rice barked, tugging on his bushy mustache.

Eos and Ligon exchanged troubled glances as the officer

issued a voice command to the BodComm integrated in his armor. A vid interface projected into the space in front of him. The feed from a drone camera began to play, and a dense grove of verdant trees flashed by. Eos was startled to see that the air in the southern region of Sutorax was clear.

The drone ducked beneath the tightly packed canopy, and Eos's mouth fell open at the staggering beauty of the lush, diverse landscape that opened up. Brightly feathered birds with long, curved bills hovered as they fed on the nectar in swathes of flowering vines draped between a myriad of emerald-colored trees on the steep slopes. The birds called to each other in short, sharp, high-pitched chirps unfamiliar to Eos.

Ferns, shrubs, mosses, sedges, and grasses of every shade of green mantled the floor beneath. Nothing here was coated in the dust that rendered their town a sickly variation of gray in every season. Evidently, the many layers of vegetation in the vast forest blunted the corrosive effects of the rain.

Eos almost gasped out loud when the drone flew past a trio of shimmering waterfalls plummeting like a wall of tears from the crestline down the steep forest slopes. A thunderous crashing filled her ears.

"Coming up now, sir," the officer said, clearing his throat with a hint of pride.

Eos felt a strange thrumming in her chest. Whatever secretive piece of footage they were about to view, it must contain something even more spectacular than what they had already witnessed, if that were possible. She raised a questioning brow at Ligon. He shrugged, looking every bit as bewildered as she felt.

The drone slowed to a crawl as though monitoring something, and Eos searched the interface, trying to decipher what it had observed. Her fingers dug into Ligon's arm. The swaying greenery beneath the hovering drone was actually a group of pale, thin, diaphanous creatures! They were moving, *walking*—blending in to their surroundings like chameleons. Seconds later, sensing an invader loitering above them, they vanished in a flutter of limbs and the vid interface faded out.

Admiral Rice swore loudly, his thick arms folded across his chest. "I told the top brass they'd get their biodiverse jackpot if they gave me enough time. That footage should be more than adequate to secure our funding into the next year. Transmit the feed to HQ ASAP." He activated his BodComm and began recording as he strode toward the warehouse doors. "Native population sighting confirmation. A reclusive hairless biped that stands over seven feet tall with a light green thorax and abdomen resembling a giant beetle. Stand by for vid feed." He wheeled around to address the officer again. "From now on, I want twenty-four-hour drone surveillance. I need an accurate and reliable species assessment as soon as possible."

"Yes, sir!" The officer saluted and clipped his heels together before following Admiral Rice out of the warehouse. The rolling steel doors clanged shut, leaving Eos and Ligon alone once again in the shadows.

Eos sank back on the cold floor, tingling all over. "Can you believe it? That was insane!"

Ligon set his lips in a grim line. "Eos, you can't even hint at this to anyone. If the military finds out we know about this, we're going to be in serious trouble."

Eos slid him a disgruntled look. "The only person who'll be in trouble once this goes viral is the idiot maintenance worker who missed the mysteriously growing hole in the perimeter fence."

"I mean it, Eos." Ligon grabbed her arms, his eyes flashing

a mixture of irritation and fear. "This isn't just about us. I have my mother and Marfa to think about. Who's going to provide for them if anything happens to me?"

"All right, all right, I get it," Eos said, softening at the unease in his voice. "I won't say anything to anyone, *yet*. But, you have to admit, this is the most amazing thing that's ever happened!"

Ligon released his grip on her, his expression relaxing. "What do you think they are, some kind of animal?"

"You heard the admiral—*native population*. Bona fide aliens. First time they've seen a drone, I'm guessing. They bolted when they sensed it overhead."

"Animals sense things too," Ligon pointed out.

Eos raised her brows. "I guess they could be some unknown species of animal, but they're obviously intelligent."

"Not that intelligent—they've never attempted to make contact with us."

"How do you know that? Maybe the settlers are being kept in the dark about them." Eos reached for her backpack. "The military shouldn't be hiding this from us. We have a right to know what's out there. Sutorax is our home, too."

"Not for much longer if we're discovered on the base," Ligon responded. "Let's get out of here."

They made quick work of selling their finds at the market before it closed for the day. Scrap metal was in high demand now that steel production on Sutorax had shut down—the emissions' impact on the deteriorating environment had been deemed too toxic.

Ligon was unusually jovial on the way home, peppering Eos with goofy jokes in his best alien accent. "What … is … that … unidentified … frying … object … you … are … cooking … mother?"

Eos rolled her eyes and smiled to herself as she fingered the DigiBand on her wrist, flush with fresh credits—more than she had made in the past six months. Marfa would have all the medication she needed now. And her mother would have a birthday present this year that surpassed all her expectations.

Inside the sanitation foyer at her apartment, Eos shrugged out of her protection suit and headed into the tiny kitchen where her mother was bent over the infusion cooktop stirring a pot of soup. Eos hugged her tightly from behind.

"How was your Solday?" her mother asked. The smile she flicked Eos's way didn't quite reach her eyes as she proceeded to whisk the soup into a froth. Eos frowned, picking up on her mother's thinly camouflaged tension. "What's wrong? Did something happen to father?"

Her mother sighed and tossed aside the ladle in her hand. "No. My department is closing. After this week, I won't have a job anymore." Her eyes welled with tears. "The rent is due in a few days. And our debts are mounting. We can't possibly make it on your father's salary alone—I don't even know how much longer we can depend on that. His cough has been getting worse lately."

Eos's chest tightened as she digested the news. They had already downsized to a cramped apartment in a less desirable area of town to cut costs. Other than the slums, there was nothing cheaper available on Sutorax. What if her father grew too sick to work? She swallowed hard, the credits in her DigiBand burning into her wrist. Her mother's birthday present would have to wait for another year.

"Don't worry about the rent," Eos reached for her mother's wrist and deftly transferred the credit balance from her DigiBand to her mother's.

"Where did you get this?" Her mother's brow wrinkled in confusion as she stared down at her DigiBand.

"I salvaged some scrap metal and parts and resold them at the market. I was saving up to buy you something special for your birthday, but ..."

Her mother pressed a hand to her mouth and suppressed a sob. "Thank you, Eos."

"Will it be enough?"

Her mother wiped the back of her sleeve over her face. "Between this and the little bit of savings we have, and your father's paycheck, we can pull the rent together for this month. After that, I don't know what we'll do."

Eos hugged her mother again, pasting on a comforting smile. She wouldn't make her any promises she couldn't keep. It had taken her over six months to save what she had. Still, she would redouble her salvaging efforts next Solday. And she would risk a return trip to the base, with or without Ligon.

When the CommAmp announced the commencement of classes at the AcademPlex on Monday morning, Ligon tugged Eos aside. "Remember, not a hint to anyone."

Eos twisted her lips into a wry grin and stuck a hand on her hip. "Excuse me, Dr. Rossdale, has anyone ever discovered archaeological evidence of an earlier settlement on Sutorax—skinny, hairless, green people, perhaps?"

Ligon laughed as he shushed her, then snuck a glance over her shoulder to make sure no one had overheard them. "*Especially* not in Dr. Rossdale's science class. If anyone's going to ask questions, it'll be him."

"Ligon! Eos!"

They swiveled in tandem at the grating sound of Principal Hale's voice.

"In my office, now, please."

Eos's ears filled with pounding fear. Surely Principal Hale couldn't have overheard them from inside her office? Eos slid Ligon a glance, and he gave a slight shake of his head warning her not to say anything more. Her throat tightened. She should never have mentioned the skinny, green people. Their conversation might have been recorded by a hidden device. Her legs made spastic movements as she followed Ligon down the corridor and into the principal's office.

Principal Hale gestured in a flustered fashion to the adjoining conference room, her groomed brows slashed together in a perturbed frown. "There are some people here to see you."

Eos sucked in a breath. Had something happened—to her father, or Marfa? She exchanged a questioning look with Ligon as they made their way inside the conference room. Principal Hale closed the door quietly behind them.

Eos's eyes widened when Admiral Rice rose to greet them. A slew of rapid-fire questions flooded her brain. What was the admiral doing at the AcademPlex? How come he only wanted to speak to her and Ligon? And why was Principal Hale so agitated?

The admiral shot out a burly hand to Eos. "Pleasure to meet you." His grip almost crushed the bones in her fingers. He shook hands with Ligon also, and then gestured to the officer standing at attention on his right. "This is Officer Munson, my second-in-command."

Eos stared at Officer Munson as she sank down in a swivel chair, but it was impossible to read anything from his stony expression. Her hands shook in her lap. It couldn't be just a coincidence that the military had shown up at the AcademPlex the day after she and Ligon had been trespassing on the base.

Admiral Rice glanced at the DigiBand on his wrist and then looked up sharply. "I won't waste your time with preamble. The reason I requested this meeting is to recruit both of you to our elite cadet training program."

Eos furrowed her brow, turning the words over in her mind. They rang hollow. Alarms bells were going off in her head. The military didn't recruit settlers. All the officers came from HQ and were transferred around the colonization ring as needed. A neutral force with no allegiance to any one planet over another. Her throat felt dry when she tried to speak. "I ... didn't know the military had a cadet program."

Admiral Rice fiddled with his mustache, eying her with an air of cunning. "Admittedly, it's a new program. You will be our first students. You will live and train on the base."

"I appreciate the offer, sir," Ligon said, bobbing his knee nervously. "But my mother and sister rely on me to help support them. My sister has respiratory problems and needs medication."

"I can assure you that won't be an issue." The admiral gave a dismissive wave of his hand. "Your monthly stipend will be more than enough to provide for them, and, as a military family, all future medical expenses will be covered."

A bewildered frown flickered across Ligon's brow. He opened his mouth and then shut it again, as though second-guessing his response.

"We'll still need to discuss it with our parents." Eos slid forward in her seat, hoping to signal her intention to return to class.

Admiral Rice raised a hand to stop her before she stood.

"We have already conferred with your parents. Everything's been taken care of. They are in full agreement." He tapped the DigiBand on his wrist and projected a static interface into the space between them. Eos scanned the enlistment contract in front of her, blood pumping furiously in her temples. She studied her parents' signatures at the bottom of the form. Her stomach muscles tightened.

They had given their permission for the military to requisition Eos as an *asset*. What did that even mean? The verbiage unnerved her. Assets could be used up, depleted, squandered. She bit her lip as the interface faded from view.

"Why did you select us for the program?" Ligon asked, his tone laced with suspicion.

Something shifted in the admiral's expression. "Let's just say you have exhibited above-average skills in areas deemed beneficial to the military."

Ligon shook his head and got to his feet abruptly, the legs of his chair scraping across the tile floor. "I'm sorry, I can't accept your offer. I don't care what my mother signed. My sister depends on me for more than just credits."

Admiral Rice tilted his head in Officer Munson's direction. Without a word, the officer activated his BodComm, and a vid interface materialized in front of them. Ligon sank back down, his face paling.

Eos watched the footage of two shadowy figures in personal protection suits skulking along the side of the warehouse on base—unmistakably her and Ligon. They had unwittingly looked up at a hidden camera before they went through the access door into the warehouse. Eos's skin prickled with fear.

Admiral Rice sighed and leaned back in his chair, interlacing his thick fingers. "The time stamp on the perimeter camera puts both of you inside the warehouse yesterday at the same time I was there."

The pulse in Eos's throat throbbed so violently she could hardly hear herself think. "Oh," she said, a tad too breathlessly to project innocence. Beads of sweat prickled along her hairline.

Admiral Rice's narrowed eyes bored into her before he turned his attention to Ligon. "I was reviewing classified reconnaissance footage with one of my officers." He drummed his fingers on the table. "Unfortunately, it turns out there were two extra pairs of eyes in the warehouse that day."

Ligon scowled.

"So, now you understand my dilemma." Admiral Rice's lips split in a feral grin. "I could have you expelled from the AcademPlex for entering the restricted zone. However, I have decided that an alternative course of action might prove beneficial to both parties. This way, you get to finish your education, and the military gains two cadets who can be trained to handle some of the entry-level tasks around the base that have suffered due to recent budget cuts." The admiral paused and cocked his head to one side. "And then, of course, there are your parents to consider. Your new stipends would undoubtedly relieve their financial burdens considerably."

"When ... would we have to begin?" Eos asked.

Admiral Rice slapped the desk and stood. "Today. Now. Officer Munson and I are here to escort you to the base.

Outfitted in crisp, new, black military protection suits, Eos and Ligon waited outside Admiral Rice's office on base for further instructions. The shock of what had transpired over the last couple of hours was only now beginning to sink in.

"He's afraid we're going to leak their secret," Eos said. "He made up the whole cadet program so he could keep the existence of the aliens under wraps."

"He can't make us stay here forever," Ligon muttered. He cast a nervous glance up at the ceiling, checking for microphones.

"He can keep us here for as long as it takes the military to admit there are aliens on Sutorax," Eos huffed. "We could be stuck here for months."

The door to the office swung open and Admiral Rice strode out, accompanied by Officer Munson.

The admiral ran an appraising eye over Eos and Ligon's new suits. "Tuck your pant legs into your boots. First rule of business on the base is never to make a sloppy impression."

He waited for them to comply and then marched them out of the administrative building and across the yard to a transit vehicle parked nearby.

Eos and Ligon climbed into the back seat and sat in silence as a wooden-faced Officer Munson drove them and the admiral across the base to the hangars.

"What are we doing here?" Ligon asked, a note of apprehension in his voice.

"You stuck your nose into this mission," Admiral Rice said, climbing out. "Now, you get to participate."

Officer Munson gestured at Ligon and Eos to get out and follow the admiral to the nearest hangar.

A large group of officers and scientists were already assembled inside. A current of anticipation pervaded the atmosphere. The admiral walked to the front of the crowd and faced them, folding his hands behind his back.

"Today, we fly our first mission to initiate contact," he announced.

A rumble of excitement went around the room.

"Once our drones locate the bipeds, we will make a drop of a mobile BodComm preloaded with a short vid in which I will introduce myself and explain the purpose of our colony, and then we'll monitor the bipeds' response," the admiral continued. "Our researchers will assess the initial findings and advise us on the intellectual capacity of the species. Any questions?"

"No, sir," the officers and scientists chorused.

The admiral nodded, satisfied. "Return to your stations."

As it turned out, it was almost a month later before the drones located the green creatures again. A month during which Eos and Ligon underwent vigorous weaponry and tactical training, but for what purpose they weren't entirely sure. They were cadets, not officers, but they had yet to be assigned any of the menial tasks around the base that Admiral Rice had alluded to.

They were hanging up their gear after a particularly exhausting weaponry session, when word spread throughout the base that the aliens had finally been spotted again. Along with everyone else not working directly on the mission, they raced to the conference room to watch the raw footage.

Eos stared, heart racing, as the elongated, green creatures came into view on the vid feed. They moved as a synchronized whole, a latticework of limbs that mimicked the forest, not easy to spot at first. When the drone began to descend, they scattered, dissolving into the greenery like before. The drone hovered low to the ground and dropped a basket before ascending and continuing to film from above.

For several minutes, Eos detected no sign of the aliens. Then, a sudden glint of green reappeared in the vid feed like dye shooting through water. Gradually, the willowy creatures' outlines sharpened back into focus. Eos held her breath when one of them broke away from the group and advanced toward the basket. Its fluid, graceful movements made it seem as though it were one with the atoms it moved through. It extended long, cadaverous fingers and scooped up the BodComm from the basket, triggering the remote activation of a vid interface.

Admiral Rice appeared in the feed, regal in full dress uniform and military cap. He smiled broadly and pointed to his chest as he introduced himself. The camera in the drone zoomed in on the expression on the green creature's face. It exhibited no fear of the vid feed—no curiosity either, although Eos had a hunch it was deceptively intelligent. She studied the luminescent network of yellow veins in its peculiar eyes, wondering how much it understood of what it was seeing. The creature's pupils were glistening ovals of darkness, and she couldn't tell what emotion lurked within, if any.

A collective gasp went around the conference room when the creature skillfully strapped the BodComm around its abdomen and rejoined the rest of its group. A subtle rippling of green blurred together on the feed, and then the aliens vanished again.

Admiral Rice grinned around the room. "Clearly, they are sentinel beings. And their actions demonstrate acceptance of our overtures to befriend them. Our next step will be to initiate contact on the ground."

Eos listened enthralled as Admiral Rice detailed the strategy. "The test subjects selected to make first contact will be lowered from a supply craft through the tree canopy in a bulletproof cube designed by HQ for this very purpose. Once it has been established that the aliens mean no ill will, the cube will be remotely opened and the test subjects will be released to make contact with the creatures."

A chorus of questions filled the room.

"What if the aliens exhibit hostility?"

"What if the test subjects are captured?"

"Or eliminated?"

Admiral Rice waved the questions aside impatiently. "HQ has reviewed the footage and ordered us to send down both a male and a female subject. The hope is that including a female of our species will lower the risk of hostility in the aliens, and also aid us in determining if there is more than one sex among them, despite their androgynous appearance."

"How will the test subjects be selected?" an officer asked.

Admiral Rice's calculating gaze roamed the room and

INTERCEPTION

then homed in on Eos and Ligon. "Our elite cadets will make first contact."

Eos gripped the edges of her seat as the words harpooned her gut. She flicked a frightened glance at Ligon.

"They can't make us," he murmured, the color leaching from his face.

"This was his plan all along." Eos clenched her jaw. "He tricked our parents with his bogus cadet program. If we die at the aliens' hands, you can bet they won't see a single credit."

She looked around the room nervously. All eyes latched onto her and Ligon. She needed to stop this madness now before it went any further.

"We're not equipped for first contact. We're not trained officers," she protested.

"Which is precisely why you're expendable assets," Admiral Rice retorted. "Skilled military from HQ are impossible to replace under the current budget restrictions." He snapped his fingers and several officers materialized around Eos and Ligon.

"Prep the cadets for contact. We leave in forty-eight hours," the admiral ordered, before exiting the conference room, leaving Eos and Ligon numb with shock.

Officer Munson spent most of the next two days coaching Eos and Ligon on HQ's protocol for initiating alien contact and conducting any subsequent interaction. "Eos, you will lead off the conversation," he said, in the final briefing before the supply craft was due to depart. "The female of the species is typically perceived as less threatening, so we'll run with that thesis until proven otherwise. And remember to remove your sunglasses as soon as you exit the cube so that the aliens can see your eyes. It will make you seem more trustworthy. HQ's ultimate goal is to secure a specimen of the species, and it will be better for everyone if we can persuade one of them to accompany us voluntarily."

"You might have trained for these scenarios back at HQ," Eos grumbled. "But we're just kids. We haven't even graduated from the AcademPlex yet. How are we supposed to know if the interaction is becoming too dangerous, or if the aliens are about to attack?"

"We'll have weapons aimed on them at all times," Officer Munson reassured her. "At the first sign of hostile intent, we will take them out for your protection."

"The pulse beams could go right through them," Ligon said. "You don't even know what these aliens are made of. They appear and disappear like ghosts."

Officer Munson threw him an apologetic look. That was, after all, why Ligon and Eos had been selected to initiate contact. They were *expendable*, as Admiral Rice had put it.

"Our scientists surmise they are made up of a frame and connective tissue just as we are." Officer Munson hesitated. "We have every reason to believe our weapons will be effective." He got to his feet. "It's time to transfer you to the hangar for departure."

Eos climbed with leaden feet into the supply craft after Ligon. In addition to Admiral Rice and Officer Munson, the first contact team consisted of an anthropologist, a linguist, and two plasma-beam snipers. They would be backed up by a second military craft equipped with cannon firepower and a squadron of officers, although Eos seriously doubted the military would attempt a ground rescue if things went downhill.

She wondered what her parents would think if they could see her now. They would never have agreed to sign her up for this if they had known the danger it would put her in. She suspected they hadn't been told much about the phony cadet program. Maybe they thought she had been sent to train at HQ. Regardless, there was no hope of them coming to her aid. If she and Ligon survived this alien encounter, it would be due to their own ingenuity.

Ligon slid into the seat next to her. "Probably stupid to ask if you're ready for this?"

Eos arched a brow. "I missed the training module on how not to present as alien bait."

Ligon sighed. "That's pretty much what we'll be in that cube, chum for the green feeders—and all because we salvaged a few scrap parts from the base."

"It seemed like a good idea at the time," Eos said apologetically. "I never figured we'd end up as expendable assets." She stared glumly out the window as their craft sped south toward Sutorax's heavily forested region. Whatever death lay in store for them would be wholly unnatural, although she particularly dreaded the thought of being eaten alive. Of course, there was always the comforting alternative that maybe the aliens would keep them as pets.

The supply craft slowed on approach to the coordinates where the green creatures had last been spotted and hovered in position over a small opening in the tree canopy.

Officer Munson directed Ligon and Eos into the cube at the back of the craft and positioned them for landing.

"Stick to the protocol," Admiral Rice reminded them. "Avoid inflammatory exchanges. Your mission is simply to gather intelligence."

Eos glared at him. "And return intact."

Ignoring her jibe, he gave the command to lower them to the ground.

Eos and Ligon jerked sideways when the underbelly of the craft opened up and the translucent cube began a controlled descent on a steel cable. Eos slipped her fingers over Ligon's hand. "Please don't hate me for getting you into this."

Ligon's eyes widened. "I could never hate you." He squeezed her hand playfully. "Of course, you're still mildly irritating, mind-blowingly reckless, and you slurp your tea, in case you hadn't noticed."

Eos forced a grin. "In a word, irresistible?"

A smile played on Ligon's lips.

For a moment, Eos actually thought he might be about to lean forward and kiss her, but then the cube landed on the mossy floor with a deadening thud.

Eos and Ligon remained frozen in place, eyes locked on one another. Tentatively, Eos shifted her gaze to the thickly forested slopes around them, searching for movement, a barely perceptible green flicker that would let her know the elusive creatures had witnessed their arrival. Her chest was so tight as she scanned the foliage that she could scarcely force a breath from it.

She blinked, and suddenly the aliens materialized in her line of vision, not thirty feet from the cube, ramrod straight and looking right at them. Her insides contracted in a coil of fear.

"Don't move," Ligon said, breathing heavily in her ear. "Let's see if they approach us."

They waited, eyes glued on the creatures who held their stance, silent and unflinching, like giant stick insects.

Crackling erupted in their BodComms and Admiral Rice's voice filtered through. "Looking good so far. We're going to proceed with the next step of the plan and open the cube. Remain calm. We don't want to startle them."

Eos took a deep, cleansing breath, trying to reassure herself that nothing horrific was going to happen. The aliens weren't armed. That meant they came in peace, right? Then again, maybe they didn't need weapons to tear their prey apart.

"Do you think it hurts to be eaten alive?" she whispered to Ligon.

He narrowed his eyes at her. "'Mildly irritating' was an understatement."

Before she could respond, the sides of the cube collapsed outward onto the moss with a soft plopping sound. She froze, afraid the noise might incite the creatures to attack, but they remained immobile. Maybe the footage of Admiral Rice on the BodComm they had retrieved had reassured them to some degree that humans were harmless.

"Now, slowly begin your approach," Admiral Rice instructed. "I won't be directing the operation anymore once you reach the aliens, so adhere to the protocol we went over."

Gingerly, Eos and Ligon got to their feet, never taking their eyes off the reedy, iridescent creatures.

"Ready?" Ligon asked.

Eos nodded, without looking at him.

Side-by-side they trod steadily toward the aliens; thirty feet, twenty-five, twenty, fifteen ...

All of a sudden, something flickered like a green silk scarf unfurling, and then they were surrounded. Eos stiffened, her entire body resonating one giant note of fear. It was impossible to retreat to the landing cube now. They were completely at the aliens' mercy.

For some strange reason, Dr. Rossdale's face flashed to mind, and Eos wondered what he would do in her situation. Would he be more fascinated than afraid? As a scientist, what would he observe first?

Eos's eyes darted left and right, but none of the creatures made a move to bridge the remaining four-foot gap between them. She told herself it was stupid to fear that the creatures would eat them. Up close, their lipless mouths were tiny—

not much bigger than a fingernail—unless their jaws could extend like the boa constrictors Dr. Rossdale had told them about back on Earth. A shiver ran across her shoulders. Thankfully, the aliens' limbs appeared far too spindly to crush her, but Officer Munson had repeatedly warned her and Ligon that their apparent lack of strength might be deceptive.

"Get rid of your sunglasses," Ligon muttered in her ear.

Eos hurriedly pulled them off and stuffed them into her jacket pocket. She was supposed to lead off the conversation, but in her panic, she had forgotten all the questions she was meant to ask. She winced as she thought of Admiral Rice pounding his fist in the cockpit, his face reddening with rage as she botched first contact.

In the end, it was Ligon who spoke first.

"My ... name ... is ... Ligon." He enunciated each word slowly, tapping his fingers to his chest as he spoke.

Forcing herself into gear, Eos stretched out her hand to the creature opposite her. It mimicked her movement, its long fingers wrapping all the way around hers. Its grip was so cold Eos almost cried out in pain. Gritting her teeth, she tapped her other hand to her chest.

"I'm Eos. What is your name?"

Heart pounding, she watched, fascinated, as the alien's minuscule mouth shaped a word.

"We have no need of names," it said in a bubbling tone that made it sound as if all the creatures were talking at once.

Eos peered around at them, each one standing at precisely the same height as the next, identical in form, bereft of any distinguishing marks. Not even a necklace or a piercing as a gesture of individuality. Curiosity overpowered her fear.

"How do you tell each other apart?" she asked. It wasn't a

question on the intelligence-gathering script they had practiced ad nauseam, but she wanted to know.

"Names are unnecessary. You are talking to any one of us." The line of green figures blurred for a brief second as they switched places at a blindingly fast pace. Eos was left staring at the same creature she had been talking to a moment earlier. Or was it? She shook her head to clear her thoughts.

She threw a furtive glance at Ligon. She couldn't imagine a world in which he was her double. The idea of never again experiencing those tiny ripples of pleasure she got when she looked at him was downright depressing.

Eos turned her attention back to the creature now standing in front of her. "Don't you ever try to look just a little different from one another?" she probed. "You know, hang some shells around your neck, stick a flower behind your ear or something."

"We are content to replicate a common form, as are most species," the creature replied. "You are an invasive species. You do not assimilate. You mutate and modify."

"How do you know about us?" Eos flinched when her tone came out harder than she had intended.

"We know you have disturbed the ecological balance on Sutorax."

Eos frowned. "You mean the dust clouds?"

"Your actions called them up," the creature said.

Ligon tugged discreetly on Eos's sleeve. "Don't upset them," he whispered.

"I'm not trying to!" Eos hissed back.

"There is always discord when two of your species talk," the creature said. "I will converse with only one of you."

Eos and Ligon exchanged unsettled looks.

"Go ahead," Ligon mumbled.

Eos nodded distractedly and turned her attention back to the creature opposite her. "Who is your leader?"

The alien's eyes contracted, the dark ovals narrowing to dashes so briefly that Eos almost thought she imagined it.

"A leader is a construct required by an unharmonious species. We have no need of a leader. We are one consciousness."

Eos blinked, taken aback by the notion that any one of the creatures standing here could read the others' thoughts. Or maybe they all had the same thoughts, so there was nothing to read. It would certainly simplify things. Humans seemed to spend half their lives trying to guess what other people were thinking. Yet, wasn't that what made interacting with others interesting—having something to discover?

The creature's gaze burrowed into her. "Does your leader have no desire to meet with us?"

"He's waiting for us in the craft," Ligon explained.

"It's not that he didn't want to meet you," Eos added hastily. "He just wanted us to make sure it would be all right with you first."

The alien interlaced its stem-like fingers in front of its thorax. "Return to your craft and send him to us."

Eos arched a brow in Ligon's direction. "Uh, okay, we can do that."

"Nice meeting you all," Ligon said with a quick wave.

When the creature didn't respond, Eos and Ligon turned and made their way back to the cube, careful not to appear overly eager to make their escape for fear some undisclosed predatory instincts might kick in, despite the aliens' apparent docile nature.

When they reached the cube, they positioned themselves inside it and Ligon relayed instructions to Officer Munson to seal the sides and winch them up. They sat in silence, mentally replaying every detail of their bizarre encounter with the aliens as the cube steadily ascended and breached the tree line.

Once they were safely back inside the belly of the supply craft, Officer Munson released the cube's sides and reached out to give them a helping hand to their feet. Eos accepted gratefully, her legs wobbling beneath her, adrenalin seeping from her pores.

"Good work," Admiral Rice grunted, towering over them.

"Did you get all that?" Ligon wiped the sweat from his brow. "They want to meet you."

The admiral nodded, smoothing out his mustache.

"What are you going to do, sir?" Officer Munson asked.

"It would be remiss of me to pass up this opportunity to gather additional intelligence for HQ. I'm going down there. They've demonstrated by their actions and words that they're peace-loving beings."

Officer Munson looked unconvinced. "They called us an invasive species for not assimilating. And they blame us for disturbing the ecological balance."

"Their tone was not hostile, merely instructional," the anthropologist interjected. "It was an observation on their part."

"Do you want us to go back down?" Eos asked.

Admiral Rice shook his head. "No, they're done with you. They made it clear they wanted to speak to your leader. I need to take it from here."

"Make sure to ask how they are able to understand us," the linguist piped up.

Admiral Rice nodded and checked his BodComm. "Keep the weapons trained on them, but do not fire under any circumstances, unless I give the order."

"Understood, sir," Officer Munson replied. "We'll have the craft on standby for a rapid departure, just in case."

Admiral Rice hesitated in the doorway of the craft. "This

discovery of an indigenous population on one of the colonization planets will undoubtedly propel us to fame back in HQ, so keep your wits about you, and don't let this become a blood bath just because one of you gets spooked."

"Yes, sir," the officers replied.

Admiral Rice climbed inside the landing cube and settled into position as the sides sealed around him. "Good to go," he mouthed, giving a thumbs-up. Officer Munson saluted and began lowering the cube beneath the tree canopy.

Eos and Ligon turned their attention to the screen in the cockpit to follow the admiral's progress. Once on the ground, he waited for several minutes to make sure his arrival hadn't envoked any hostility on the part of the green creatures. When they made no advances toward him, he gave the order to open the cube.

Eos stared transfixed as Admiral Rice approached the shimmering green group. As before, the creatures exhibited no sign of fear or aggression, no emotion of any kind, for that matter. Maybe it went along with the sameness they prided themselves on. Still, Eos scarcely dared to breathe when Admiral Rice stuck out his hand and introduced himself.

"Beautiful part of the planet you live in," he commented, looking admiringly at the steeply forested slopes around them. "How many of you live here?" His tone was deliberately casual, but Eos knew the question was a critical part of the intelligence-gathering she had glossed over.

"As many as are needed," the creature said in a warbling tone that hinted at thousands of voices harmonizing with one another.

Eos could tell the answer made the admiral uneasy. He threw a quick glance over his shoulder to make sure more green creatures weren't multiplying around him.

"You all look about the same age," the admiral continued in a genial tone. "How old are you?"

"That is as absurd as asking how green I am," the alien replied.

Admiral Rice shifted his stance and rubbed his jaw, momentarily thrown from his script. "I tend to agree with you. Age is mostly irrelevant." He gave a stilted smile. "You met my two youngest recruits earlier—a male and a female cadet. May I ask how many sexes your species has?"

"How many sexes? How many years? How many beings? You seek only to understand by numbers."

"It's kind of how we do things where I'm from," Admiral Rice admitted, scratching the back of his neck. "But, forget the numbers for now. I'm curious how you're able to understand our language?"

"We understand the symbolism behind language. From there, it is a simple process to decipher what is being said."

Admiral Rice raised his beefy brows. "Impressive—kind of like a built-in translator of sorts." He wet his lips and looked around the group. "Do any of you have questions for me?"

Before the creatures could respond, the footage flickered and the audio cut out. A moment later, the vid feed flat lined.

Officer Munson jumped to his feet, swearing loudly. "Cannons at the ready! I need eyes on the admiral, now! Get that connection back up ASAP!"

The snipers kept their plasma guns aimed through the dense tree canopy in the direction where they last saw the group. Seconds later, the feed resumed, and Admiral Rice came back into view.

"Stand down," Officer Munson relayed via BodComm to the backup military craft, the relief in his voice apparent. "The admiral's safe—still in conversation with the aliens."

Eos let out a long breath, relieved as much for her own

sake as for the admiral's. Her fate and Ligon's was in his hands. If he disappeared, they might never be allowed to return home.

"Looks like he's getting ready to leave," Ligon said, pointing at the screen.

They watched as Admiral Rice shook hands with the creature in front of him and then replaced his sunglasses before walking back to the cube.

"He's good," Officer Munson said. "Seal it up and reel him in."

The snipers remained in position, their guns trained on the opening in the tree canopy on the off chance the aliens might come flying through at any minute in hot pursuit.

To everyone's relief, Admiral Rice made it back to the craft without incident. The officers burst into spontaneous applause when he exited the cube.

Eos bit her shaking lip. First contact had been a success. Maybe their performance would be enough to secure their release, and she and Ligon could finally go home. After today's incredible accomplishment, Admiral Rice would surely be compelled to reveal the existence of the aliens to the settlers. There would no longer be any reason to confine them to the base.

Officer Munson saluted the admiral. "Well done, sir. Mission accomplished."

Admiral Rice nodded, sank down in the seat next to Eos, and buckled in as the supply craft accelerated away from the dense forest canopy.

"What's our next step?" Eos asked.

Admiral Rice removed his glasses and turned to her. "Assimilation."

Her heart shuddered to a stop.

The yellow-veined eyes looking back at her were flawless ovals of darkness.

THE END

Check out my award-winning science fiction thriller *Girl of Fire: The Expulsion Project Book One* on Amazon!

The path to revolution has a twist...
...for a runaway Chieftain's daughter and an indentured serf who has never known a day of freedom. Adrift a ramshackle mining vessel, they uncover a dark secret that leads them to the brink of war.
Stakes rise when a barbaric space pirate crosses their path and a shocking discovery plunges them headlong into a frantic race against time and space to destroy the genocidal Artificial Intelligence that has taken over their planet.

- *A betrayal they never expected.*
- *A love they never anticipated.*
- *A war they were never supposed to win.*

Their world is doomed and only they can save it. Will Trattora and Velkan navigate the treacherous dealings of the seedy Galactic underworld in time to rescue the ones they love?
If you like sci-fi dystopian thrillers with a whisper of romance, a heavy dose of adventure, and action galore, then you'll love Girl of Fire! Teens and adults alike are raving about this fast-paced Galactic saga hurtling through space and danger! If you are a Firefly or Dark Matter fan, this is the book for you!

Grab your copy now for a captive read you won't want to put down!

★★★★★ *Winner 2017 National Indie Excellence Award for Young Adult Fiction*

★★★★★ *Gold Medalist 2017 Reader's Favorite Young Adult Sci-fi*

★★★★★ *2017 IPPY National Silver Medalist Young Adult Fiction*

★★★★★ *Semi-finalist 2017 Kindle Book Awards*

BIOGRAPHY

NYT and USA Today bestselling author Norma Hinkens writes psychological suspense thrillers, as well as fast-paced science fiction and fantasy about spunky heroines and epic adventures in dangerous worlds. She's also a travel junkie, legend lover, and idea wrangler, in no particular order. She grew up in Ireland, land of make-believe and the original little green man.

Find out more about her books on her website.
www.normahinkens.com

Follow her on Facebook for funnies, giveaways, cool stuff & more!

BOOKS BY NORMA HINKENS

I also write young adult science fiction and fantasy thrillers under Norma Hinkens.

www.normahinkens.com/books

THE UNDERGROUNDERS SERIES - POST-APOCALYPTIC
Immurement
Embattlement
Judgement

THE EXPULSION PROJECT - SCIENCE FICTION
Girl of Fire
Girl of Stone
Girl of Blood

THE KEEPERS CHRONICLES - EPIC FANTASY
Opal of Light
Onyx of Darkness
Opus of Doom

FOLLOW NORMA:

Join her VIP Reader Club and ***get two FREE science fiction short stories!***

www.normahinkens.com

Made in the USA
Coppell, TX
25 May 2020